Fiction for Girls

by

Jane Sorenson

It's Me, Jennifer
It's Your Move, Jennifer
Jennifer's New Life
Jennifer Says Goodbye
Boy Friend
Once Upon a Friendship
Fifteen Hands
In Another Land
The New Pete
Out with the In Crowd
Another Jennifer
Family Crisis

Hi, I'm Katie Hooper
Home Sweet Haunted Home
Happy Birth Day
Honor Roll
First Job
Angels on Holiday
The New Me
Left Behind

The New Me

by Jane Sorenson

illustrated by Kathleen L. Smith

STANDARD PUBLISHING
Cincinnati, Ohio   24-03963

All Scripture quotations are from the *Holy Bible: New International Version,* © 1973, 1984 by the International Bible Society. Used by permission of Zondervan Bible Publishers and the International Bible Society.

LIBRARY OF CONGRESS
Library of Congress Cataloging-in-Publication Data

Sorensen, Jane.
    The new me! / by Jane Sorenson ; illustrated by Kathleen L. Smith.
      p.   cm. – (Katie Hooper book ; 7)
    Summary: Katie joins her best friend on a diet and tries to change her image in other ways before discovering the importance of inner beauty.
    ISBN 0-87403-563-5
    [1. Weight control–Fiction. 2. Self-perception–Fiction.
3. Friendship–Fiction. 4. Christian life–Fiction.] I. Smith,
Kathleen L., 1950- ill. II. Title. III. Series: Sorenson, Jane.
Katie Hooper book ; 7.
PZ7.S7214Nc 1989
[Fic]–dc19   89-4514
                                                          CIP
                                                          AC

To Marion and Al Whittaker

with thanks for their role modeling,
their friendship and love,
and their encouragement
of our dreams

A New Look
for Ms. Allen

"Hi, Katie!" As I reached the bus stop, Calvin Young greeted me with a huge smile. "How's my one true love?"

I grinned back. "Knock it off!" I told him. "I wonder where Sara is."

"Maybe she overslept," said Christopher Bean.

I shook my head. "Not Sara Wilcox! She's always up with the birds! I hope nothing's wrong."

The bus was late. Silently, I stood there waiting near the two boys from my homeroom.

I watched Christopher kick some dirt with his shoe. He's the tall new guy that all the girls in our room have a crush on. "Katie," he blurted out, "I was just wondering. Did you girls ever get to go skiing?"

I shook my head. "Sara and I are still saving up for our skis. How about you?"

Christopher smiled. "It's funny. I never expected to feel this way. But skiing is just as cool as surfing!"

Calvin pounded Christopher on the back. "I've never seen such a fast learner as this guy! But watch out, Old Man!" he teased. "As soon as you pass me by, I'll tell Dad to stop taking you along to Breckenridge!"

Christopher laughed. "Fat chance! Katie, your boyfriend's going to be the star of the next Winter Olympics!"

"He isn't my boyfriend!" I laughed. "Calvin's been using that line ever since kindergarten!"

Then our conversation stalled again. Mostly the boys and girls at the bus stop don't talk to each other. Now it didn't matter anyway. Because, to be honest, I couldn't think of anything else to say!

Finally, Calvin thought of something. "Hey, Katie! Have you made any chocolate chip cookies lately?"

I grinned. "Why? Is that the only reason you like me?" I teased.

"They say good cooking is the way to a man's heart!" Christopher smiled. "Maybe it's true! Remember when we all ate cookies at your house and studied for our spelling test!"

8

I decided to brag a little. "For your information, I really am a good cook! Cookies aren't the only thing I can make!"

"Now I know I'm in love!" Calvin laughed. "Want to sit with me on the bus?"

He was just kidding. Calvin Young's been teasing me like that for years! Everybody knows he always sits in the back with the guys. Just like I always sit in front with Sara.

When the bus finally came, I ended up sitting alone. Which was OK. It made me realize how nice it is to have a best friend! Although Sara Wilcox and I are in different homerooms, the rest of the time we're usually together.

I thought about the skis. I wonder if having them will be as much fun as working for them. Frankly, we might not know until next year! This winter is almost history!

I had to rush to my homeroom to keep from being tardy. "Hi, Kimberly," I said, as I slipped into my desk.

"Hi, Katie!" The tall girl smiled. It looks like she's finally starting to like Colorado!

After the bell rang, Ms. Allen smiled and said, "Good morning!" It was no big deal! The same thing happens daily in every room in the school! But something was different. I tried to figure it out.

"There are several announcements." Ms. Allen

smiled again. By now our class is used to the new teacher. Of course, we're all positive that she's the hardest one in the entire school! But down underneath we kind of like her. At least I do.

"Your mid-quarter report cards will be out next week," Ms. Allen said. Everyone groaned! "And the following week we'll be having our Valentine party!" The class cheered!

"Ms. Allen, did you know that Valentine's Day is Katie Hooper's birthday?" Calvin asked. Everybody looked at me. I could feel my face getting red.

"Then it will be a special celebration!" said Ms. Allen. She smiled right at me.

Suddenly, I figured it out! Ms. Allen's hair is different! It's real curly! And instead of her navy blue jacket, I realized that today she was wearing a pink blouse!

Well, I wasn't the only one who noticed! That's all the girls talked about at lunch!

"I wonder why Ms. Allen always wore that dumb blue jacket?" Sue Capelleti asked.

"It's called *dressing for success*," explained Kimberly Harris. "That's what career women always wear!"

"Right! Even when it's hot!" said Pam O'Grady. "I thought she'd faint those warm days when school first started!"

"I never thought I'd think of Ms. Allen as being pretty!" said Jennifer Thomas.

"Mostly it's her hair," said Michelle Davis. "She must have gotten a permanent!"

"Do you think she's stopped trying to succeed?" I asked.

"Don't be dumb, Katie!" Sue said. "I bet Ms. Allen's trying to get a boyfriend!" Everyone squealed!

Michelle's eyes got big, and she lowered her voice. "Or maybe she already has one!"

To be honest, it is very hard for me to think of teachers as being real people! I mean, for a long time I didn't even realize they have first names! But I overheard Ms. Allen introduce herself on our field trip. Her name is Alicia! Alicia Allen. Personally, I think it sounds a lot better than Ms.!

Well, curly hair or not, Ms. Alicia Allen continued to earn her reputation as a hard teacher. After lunch we had to do three whole pages of math! And another big social studies project is due on Friday!

At the end of the day, I watched to see if Ms. Allen's boyfriend showed up at school. But all I saw was Mr. Hobbs, the principal. He has a picture of his grandchildren on his desk, so I knew it couldn't be him!

As soon as I got home, I dialed Sara's number.

"Wilcox residence," said a strange voice.

"Sara, what happened? You sound awful!"

"I have a terrible cold!" she croaked.

"But you were OK yesterday!"

"I can't believe it either!" Sara moaned.

"If I had known, I'd have brought your books home," I told her. "I'll bring them tomorrow!"

"Thanks, Katie!" I could hear her blow her nose. "I look exactly like Rudolph the Red-Nosed Reindeer!"

"Can I come over?" I asked.

"Aren't you afraid you might catch it too?"

I giggled. "We share everything else!"

"I guess you could sit across the room!" she said. "But you'll have to leave before Oprah comes on!"

"Do you want me to come, or not?"

"I'm really not supposed to let anybody in. But I guess Mom probably would think you're an exception!"

"I'll be over in ten minutes!"

I rushed upstairs. My mother was dressing my baby sister Amy. I poked my head into the nursery, gave Mom a kiss, and made Amy laugh. "Sara has a bad cold," I said. "I'm going over to cheer her up!"

"Don't get too close to her," Mom said. "We've managed to stay well all winter. I hate to think of starting a round of colds now!"

I dumped my books in my room, peeled off my school clothes, and left them in a pile on my unmade bed. It took me a few minutes to find my jeans. I promised myself that as soon as I got back from Sara's I'd pick everything up!

"Why don't you take Sara some cookies?" Mom called downstairs.

"I was just getting them!" I called back. "I couldn't find a plastic bag."

As I left my house, I smiled. I couldn't wait to tell Sara all about my day. Probably because she watches so much TV, she's really into romance. So I especially couldn't wait to tell her about Ms. Allen's boyfriend!

Sara Decides to Change

To be honest, I hardly ever go over to Sara Wilcox's house. Mostly Sara and I hang out at Home Sweet Home, the old Victorian house my family moved into last summer. In general, my family is pretty laid-back. Mom's usually home when we get in from school, and she really enjoys having us around!

Frankly, Sara's four-room house is just the opposite! Although her mother is a waitress downtown and is seldom home, Mrs. Wilcox can't stand clutter! Nothing *dares* get out of place! It looks exactly like one of those model homes! Personally, although I'd never say so, I can't even imagine living there!

Sara came to the door wearing a black bathrobe and green bedroom slippers. Her nose was nearly as red as her hair!

"Hi!" I said. "I'll close the door. Don't get in a draft!" I glanced around the living room. The only thing lying around was Sara!

"I feel pathetic!" Sara moaned. "It's like somebody turned on the faucet and let the water run!"

"I'm sorry," I said. "Have you been in bed all day?"

She grinned. "Want the truth? Mostly I've been lying on the couch watching soaps!"

She knows my family doesn't even own a TV. "Was it fun?" I asked.

"Actually, when you come in in the middle of the stories, it's hard to figure out the plots," she admitted. "But in a few days, I'll probably hate going back to school!"

"Oh, my!" I said. I sounded just like my mother. "Hey, I brought you some cookies!"

"Thanks." Sara had a funny look on her face. "No offense, Katie, but I probably won't eat them. Would you mind if I gave them to my mom?"

I was surprised. "You're that sick?"

"Not really," she said. "But I made a decision today. I'm going on a diet!"

I just looked at her. I was never more astonished in my life! "A diet!" I protested. "Sara, if

16

you were any thinner, you'd be invisible!"

She giggled.

I remembered a song my mom sang. "When you pull the plug in the bathtub, you probably have to hang on so you don't slide right down the hole!"

Sara giggled some more. Then she blew her nose. "So what happened at school?"

"This morning at the bus stop, Christopher Bean thought you overslept!" I reported.

"He did?" Sara grinned. "He really missed me?"

"We all knew you weren't there," I said. "That was pretty obvious."

"So you talked to Christopher Bean?" She blew her nose.

"Not just Christopher," I explained. "You know how he always waits with Calvin!"

"Right! So you talked to both of them?"

"It was no big deal."

"Well, tell me. What did you talk about?" she asked.

"I don't remember!" I thought a minute. "Oh, Christopher asked if we've been skiing."

"He did! What did you tell him?"

"The truth," I said. "Actually, it sounds like Calvin's family takes him along to Breckenridge every week. Calvin said Christopher's getting good at skiing!"

"Wow!" said Sara. "I wonder if they'd ever consider taking us along?"

"I don't know about that. Even if they wanted to, they probably wouldn't have room in the car!"

"Youngs have a station wagon! I've seen it!" Sara said. "Anything else?"

"I don't think so. Well, they did remember the time we ate cookies at my house. And you know how Calvin teases me!"

"Katie, are you positive he isn't in love with you?" Sara asked.

I laughed. "I'm sure! It got started years ago when he found out about my birthday. He's just teasing. That's how boys act!"

"Then he isn't your boyfriend?"

"Of course not!" I said. "If I ever get a boyfriend, which I doubt, it most certainly won't be Calvin Young, who has the loudest belch in the entire school!"

Sara sighed. "I wish real life was as romantic as television!" She sneezed and blew her nose.

"Oh, I nearly forgot! Speaking of romance, something did happen today!" I grinned. "The girls in my room think Ms. Allen has a boyfriend!"

Sara's eyes got big. "Wow! Who is he?"

"It's a secret!" I said. "You don't really think she'd blab his name all over town, do you?"

18

"I guess not," Sara said. "So who told you?"

"Nobody," I said. "We figured it out! Why else would Ms. Allen get a permanent and start wearing a pink blouse?"

"You have a good point, Katie!" Sara said. "Actually, that's almost exactly what happened today on *Days of Our Lives!* When a woman decides to change her appearance, I think there's usually a man involved!"

I remembered something. "Sara, I have to ask you a question! Is that why you're going on a diet? Be honest! Do you have a boyfriend I don't know about?"

"Not yet," she said. "But I'm hoping!"

"I really don't get it!" I told her. "We've been having so much fun together! You don't need a boyfriend, Sara! You've got me!"

Sara laughed her head off. "Get real, Katie!"

I hate it when she puts me down! "You're too young to have a boyfriend anyway!" I told her.

"Not necessarily!"

I had another idea. "We can have lots of fun just watching older people! Like Ms. Allen!"

"Maybe," Sara said. "But when romance knocks on my door, I want to be ready!"

"You'll be ready!" I said. "Trust me!"

"Katie Hooper, since when did you become an expert on romance?"

"I know enough," I said. "Enough to know that

romance usually happens when you don't expect it! That's what my mother always says!"

"Do you think Ms. Allen believes that? Maybe she just wants to look good in case she meets Mr. Right!"

"Mr. Who?"

"Mr. Right. It's just an expression," she said.

"Oh."

Sara sighed. "Frankly, all day long I've been lying here like a blob watching real-life drama on TV. And not one of the heroines was fat!"

"You aren't fat!" I told her. "Why, Sara, I probably weigh lots more than you do!"

She just looked at me. She didn't say anything.

I didn't say anything either. Finally, I couldn't stand it any longer. "Tell me the truth, Sara! Do you think I'm fat?"

"Not exactly," she said. "More like plump."

Suddenly I felt my world crashing down around me! My face felt hot, and I had to take a deep breath! Being fat was something awful, something to be avoided at any cost! And I never once dreamed it could happen to me!

"Don't cry, Katie!" Sara said.

"I'm not crying!" I told her. "Give me a Kleenex. I think I'm catching your cold!"

Sara handed me a tissue. "I have an idea!" she said. "Maybe we could go on a diet together! I heard about one where all you eat is popcorn!"

I shook my head. "I don't know. It doesn't sound like anything my mother would go for!"

"But your mother isn't fat!" Sara said. "After the baby was born, she slimmed down right away!"

"That's true!" I said. "And Dad was really proud of her too! He said she looks like she did when they got married!"

"See! It's just as I thought! Men do like skinny women!"

"I don't know," I said again.

"Is Ms. Allen fa ... I mean, does she have a weight problem?"

I shook my head.

"I just think we need to be prepared," Sara said. "Unless you want to get stuck forever with Calvin Young!"

"Sara, please stop it!" I said. "I'm going home! Don't worry! I'll just take the cookies back and feed them to January!"

"You want me to be honest, don't you?" she asked.

As I put on my jacket, I nodded. "I guess so. They always say that's what friends are for!"

I Try to Face the Facts

I left Sara's house and started for Home Sweet Home. To be honest, I felt like a totally different person! I could hardly even remember my walk to Sara's, when I was so excited about seeing my friend again.

Now, what I really wanted to do was sit down and cry! But I'm too big for that. Besides, if I got my jeans all muddy, Mom would just want to know how it happened. So I just kept walking.

Never in my life have I felt so awful! My eyes kept filling with tears. And every time I brushed them away, they came right back! I could hardly breathe, and my chest felt tight. Maybe I really was getting Sara's cold!

Suddenly, I remembered the cookies. Opening

the plastic bag, I crumbled them on the ground. Then as I continued walking, I licked off the chocolate evidence from my fingers.

I know perfectly well that I'm not cool! But frankly, I don't even care! Life has always been too much fun to spend it worrying about whether my blouse is tucked in or my skirt matches!

And it's never really bothered me that I'm not a brain either. Honestly! Oh, I admire kids like Kimberly and Sara who always make the Honor Roll! But Hoopers don't have to get top grades, as long as we do our best! Actually, I think my father was more proud of my Citizen of the Month Award than if I had made straight A's!

But on the other hand, I've never thought of myself as ugly and stupid! And, to be blunt, that's how lots of people think about fat kids!

Oh, nobody actually *says* anything, at least not at school. After all, that's against the rules!

But now I wonder how I've missed the giggles and knowing looks! Is Pam O'Grady rolling her eyes with every bite of sandwich I take? Is Ms. Allen nice because she feels sorry for me? Is that why Calvin and Christopher asked me about the chocolate chip cookies?

And now the lowest blow of all! If scrawny, little Sara Wilcox is going on a diet, then my case is already hopeless!

By the time I reached my house, I was extremely depressed. Looking in the kitchen window, I saw that Mom wasn't there. I rushed in, glad I didn't have to face anybody!

As I turned on the light in my bedroom and saw the mess, all I could think of was *slob!* It's the room of someone who doesn't care! A person who doesn't really deserve the red hearts stenciled around the top of her walls!

I glanced at the row of sketches of me my father had made on each of my birthdays. In every single one, I am smiling. My sketch this year will be different. Because I know I'll never smile again! Never!

"Katie!" Mom called. "You have to set the table!"

I puffed my cheeks out and looked in the mirror. As I went downstairs, I wondered if my family knows I'm fat?

"So how's Sara doing?" Mom asked.

"She'll live," I said.

"Did you have a quarrel or something?"

"Leave me alone!" I said. "I don't want to talk about it!"

I sneaked a look at Mom standing in front of the stove. Once our baby was born, she stopped looking like a light bulb! Now, even in her apron, she stood tall and thin! She looked up at me and smiled. "I baked brownies," she said.

"I'm not hungry."

"Oh. Well that's OK. Your father and brother will eat them!"

The back door opened and Jason walked in. "Hi!" he said. "What's for supper?"

"Fried chicken!" Mom said.

"Good," Jason said. "I'm starved!"

I watched my brother take off his jacket and hang it up. Jason's almost as tall as Dad, but he weighs about a third as much! He was picked to be Joseph in the Christmas pageant because he was the only eighth grade boy taller than Jessica Hotchkiss! But even in his costume he looked skinny!

"Hi, Katie!" he said.

I looked at him and muttered, "Hi."

"What's wrong with her?" Jason asked Mom.

"Never mind!" Mom said. "Please call your father. And Katie, would you please get Amy? I think I hear her crying."

Upstairs, I took a good look at my sister. Although when she was born, Mom and Dad called her their biggest baby, she still looks pretty small to me! "You look OK so far!" I told her. "But watch out for that pudding!"

Amy grinned her toothless little smile. And I had to smile back! I couldn't help it! "Thanks!" I said. "At least somebody likes me!"

"Here come my two best girls!" Dad was waiting in the middle of the kitchen, and when I came down he enclosed both of us in his arms.

"Hi, Dad!" I smiled again.

"Put Amy in the playpen," Mom said. "Things are getting cold!"

Before we sat down, we made a circle around the table, closed our eyes, and sang: "Praise God, from whom all blessings flow; Praise Him, all creatures here below ..."

Afterwards, I watched as Dad helped Mom with her chair, then sat down himself. "It looks wonderful, Elizabeth!" he told her. "This is one of my favorite dinners!"

Sara Wilcox calls my father the Jolly Green Giant! I guess that's a pretty good description, although, of course, he isn't really green!

Now I had to smile again. Just being around Dad makes people smile! Actually, he's been large and balding as long as I can remember. But he's so graceful that I've never considered him fat! Now I watched him spear a large chicken breast and put it on his plate.

Although I usually eat a thigh, tonight I decided to find a smaller piece! I poked around until I found the heart, which was about the size of a marble! It looked pretty funny sitting there on my plate! But I couldn't laugh or somebody would notice.

No one noticed, because Mom was so busy describing the blue carpeting she found for Fellowship Hall at the church. Finally, she looked at me. "You look like you're feeling better, Katie!" She smiled.

"I'm OK." I forced a smile.

"Good," Mom said. "I hope Sara will feel better soon! That girl's so thin! Sometimes I worry about whether she's getting enough to eat!"

Suddenly, I couldn't stand it! I reached for a big piece of chicken. Before I knew it, it was gone, and Dad was asking me if I wanted another one! By dessert time, I was stuffed!

I felt so guilty that nothing mattered anyhow! And I had this incredible desire for chocolate! I knew I'd just die if I had to sit there and watch everyone else eating brownies! Believe it or not, I ended up eating two myself!

Later, as we did the dishes, Jason asked me what's wrong with Sara.

"Stop it!" I said. "That's all I ever hear anymore! Sara, Sara, Sara!"

"Well, pardon *me!*" Jason said.

I was embarrassed. For a long time I didn't say another word. Finally I put my towel down and turned to my brother. "Tell me the truth, Jason!" I said. "Have you been noticing something different about me lately?"

"As a matter of fact, I have. "Katie, is something wrong? I've never seen you so touchy!"

I Decide
to Look Cool

That night I had the worst dream. I was wandering in the halls at school. I kept opening classroom doors and starting in. But each time the kids looked up and saw me, the entire room would burst into laughter! Well, that might not sound awful to you, but I woke up in a cold sweat!

As I got out of bed, I nearly stepped on my dog January. He opened one eye and looked at me. Then he thumped his tail twice and went back to sleep.

I stood there shivering. "Get up!" I said. "I want to see you!"

January looked at me as if I were out of my mind. But slowly he rose to his feet. It must

have been the tone in my voice. Hugging myself to keep from shaking, I took a good look at him.

"Forget it!" I told him, as I headed for the bathroom. "Your fur is too thick! I guess I'll have to wait until summer to see if you're gaining weight!"

Back in my room, I stood in front of the open closet. Instead of just grabbing the first thing in sight, I selected a blue checked shirt and matching blue corduroy pants. Suddenly I remembered how pleased Mom had been when she found the outfit at the resale shop! I mean, they hardly looked as if anyone had worn them! But somehow they had ended up in the back of my closet.

"Perfect!" I said, smiling. "From now on, Katie Hooper, you're going to be the coolest girl in the entire school!"

But when I tried to fasten the pants, the button came off! I tossed them on the bed and pulled on my jeans. Being cool wasn't going to be easy! But I didn't give up. Before I went downstairs, I even brushed my hair!

Mom never noticed. "Help yourself to some oatmeal, Katie!" she said. "There are bananas on the sink. I'm going up to feed Amy."

I got all the way to the bus stop before I thought once about Sara! My friend was nowhere in sight. She was probably still sick.

Today I got no warm greeting from Calvin. He stood off to one side laughing with Christopher and another guy. Since all the girls are younger, I'm not really friends with them. To be honest, when I arrived nobody even looked up! For the second day in a row, I sat alone on the bus. Somehow, by the time I got to school, I had stopped feeling cool!

The class was already seated when Ms. Allen walked into the room. She was wearing a big smile and a red dress! Robert Jackson, who sits behind me, let out a long shrill whistle! And the other boys joined in.

"Be still my heart!" called Calvin Young.

It was the first time I'd heard Calvin teasing anyone else with his love talk. And suddenly I actually felt jealous! Of Ms. Allen! I really couldn't believe it!

Frankly, although Ms. Allen acted cool, I thought she seemed a little too pleased at all the attention! "All right, let's settle down, class!" she said.

While the teacher made announcements, I took a better look at her. Ms. Allen was wearing a pearl necklace and little pearl earrings. But the main difference was the dress. It revealed what the navy blue blazer had hidden—a shape that curved at all the right places!

Later, during math, Ms. Allen called on kids

to come to work problems at the board. Today I found myself watching people with new interest. Suddenly, I was conscious only of one thing—*how they looked!* To be more specific, I was checking to see who looked fat.

"All right, now let's have the row next to the windows come to the board," Ms. Allen said.

That's when, for the first time, I noticed Jennifer's curves! Actually, most of the girls in my room look more like ironing boards! As for myself, I decided I probably look more like a sausage!

"Wow!" Michelle said at lunch. "Who would ever have guessed Ms. Allen would have a figure like that!" Everyone giggled.

"Be honest!" Sue Capelleti said. "Do you think we'll ever look like that?"

"I sure hope so!" said Pam, giggling.

"I can't believe the boys around here are so immature!" said Kimberly. "You'd think they never saw a woman before!"

Personally, I just listened. I realized I had already eaten my whole sandwich without thinking. I looked down at the brownie. Maybe I should just leave it! Or would that be wasteful? "Anybody want my brownie?" I asked.

"I'll take it if you aren't going to eat it," said Jennifer Thomas. I tried not to stare at her tee shirt.

"I wonder if Ms. Allen really does have a boy-friend!" Michelle said. "Let's try to find out! Everybody keep an eye out! OK?"

Everyone agreed.

"And don't tell anybody!" Pam said. "It would be awful if she thought we were spying on her!"

By the time we went outside after lunch, I was pretty sure of one thing. The girls don't hate me because of my weight! I mean, if they were laughing at me, I could tell! When they chose sides for soccer, I actually was picked fourth!

When I got back after lunch, Ms. Allen asked me to come up to her desk. "Do you know some-one named Sara Wilcox?"

I nodded. "She's my best friend."

"Well, she called the principal's office to see if you'd bring home her books and assignments."

"I'll be glad to," I said.

"Katie, you look very nice today!" Ms. Allen smiled at me.

"Thank you very much!" I couldn't believe it! She actually noticed! I reached down and tucked in my shirt.

As soon as school was over, I headed off to Sara's homeroom. I had never really spoken to her teacher, Mr. Campbell. When I got there, he had her things all ready. "I hope Sara will feel better soon," he said.

"It's just a bad cold," I told him.

"Well, tell Sara we miss her!" Mr. Campbell looked at me and smiled.

Suddenly, I felt so embarrassed I thought I was going to die! "I'll tell her!" I hurried toward the door.

"Katie! You forgot Sara's books!" Mr. Campbell called after me.

Now I really felt stupid! Grabbing the books, I rushed into the hall. Then, believe it or not, I nearly knocked down Ms. Allen!

"I'm sorry!" I said. "I guess I didn't see you!"

Ms. Allen laughed. "I didn't see you either!"

"I was just getting Sara's books!"

"Oh, of course! I forgot!" Ms. Allen said. "Is she in Mr. Campbell's room?"

"Right," I said. "He's her teacher."

Ms. Allen just stood there. Naturally, she was still wearing that red dress. "Well, Katie, I hope your friend gets better soon!"

"It's just a cold," I told her.

"Don't miss your bus, Katie!" My teacher smiled at me.

She was right. I couldn't stall any longer. "See you tomorrow!" I said.

My arms full of books, I ran down the hall. But once I passed the corner, I stopped. I turned around and carefully looked back down the corridor toward Mr. Campbell's room. The hall was empty. Ms. Allen had disappeared.

I Decide
to Join Sara

When I walked into the keeping room, Mom just kept right on sewing! She never even looked up! "Have a good day?" she asked.

"Pretty good," I said. "My teacher wore a new dress."

"That's nice. There are a couple of brownies left."

"Give them to Jason," I said. "I'm going over to Sara's. She called the school and asked me to bring her books."

"Tell her I hope she feels better!"

Sara must have been watching for me, because she opened the door right away. "Hi!" she said.

"Hi! I brought your books!" I set them down on

the table and took off my jacket.

"Thanks!" She picked them up right away and carried them off into her room. I think I just discovered the secret to a neat house!

"How are you feeling?" I asked, when she returned. "You look lots better! But you sound like a foghorn!"

"My nose is better, but now it's down in my chest!" Sara seemed nervous. "Are we still friends?"

"Sure!" I smiled. "I'm OK now. Actually, you really gave me lots to think about!"

"Katie, I've been thinking. If we go on a diet together, it will be riots!"

"Are you sure?" I asked. "I've never had the impression that dieting was fun! And it takes forever!"

"It depends on the diet!" Sara grinned. "I read about one where you eat only grapefruit for a week. This one woman lost 71 pounds!"

"Impossible!" I said. "Nobody can lose 71 pounds in one week!"

"Oh," she said. "Well, maybe it was just seven pounds."

"But, Sara, if you lost seven pounds, wouldn't you be awfully skinny?"

Sara shook her head. "My face is fat! And you should see me in a bathing suit!"

"You look pretty normal to me!" I told her.

"Well, Katie, you may not realize it, but thin is very *in!*" she said. "I've noticed that thin people always look so happy! That's because they're perfect!"

"They could be happy for other reasons," I pointed out.

"Whatever! Personally, I'm interested for just one reason. I still don't have a boyfriend!"

"Neither do I! Who cares?"

"I do!" Sara said. "And I'm sure of one thing! Boys don't go out with girls that are too fat!"

I didn't know what else to say, so I didn't say anything.

"OK, Katie Hooper!" she said. "If you won't do it with me, then I'll diet alone!"

"Does it have to be grapefruit?"

"The only other diet I've heard of is the Jell-O method! But, to be honest, I don't know how to make Jell-O!"

"There's nothing to it!" I said. "I'll show you!"

Sara and I went into the Wilcox kitchen. Nothing was lying out on the counter—not even a spoon! She opened a cupboard and pulled out a package of lemon Jell-O. "At least it's something we have in the house! Can we make it in the microwave oven?"

"No," I said. "We just need a pan and a measuring cup and a stove."

Afterwards, we put the Jell-O in a bowl and

set it in the refrigerator. "Are you sure you don't want some fruit in it?" I asked. "It looks awfully plain!"

"Maybe you were right! Maybe dieting isn't supposed to be fun!" Then she giggled. "If this isn't hard by dinner time, I guess I can always drink it!"

"I've made up my mind!" I told her. "When I get home, I'll fix a bowl for myself."

"Let's start tomorrow!"

"It's a deal!" I said.

Sara led the way back to the living room. "So, what happened at school today?"

"Not much," I said. Then I grinned.

"What happened? Was it Calvin?"

"Not that dope!" I said. "Actually, I'm really not supposed to tell anybody!"

"Don't pull that! I'm your best friend!"

"Tell me what you know about Mr. Campbell," I said.

"He's so cool! A dream come true!" She rolled her eyes. "Not to mention that he's a super teacher! Why do you want to know?"

I got embarrassed. "He said everybody misses you! And he said he hopes you get well fast!"

"My pounding heart!" She put one hand on her chest and looked up at the ceiling.

"Sara, tell me something," I said. "Is Mr. Campbell married?"

"Katie, I can't believe you're asking that!"

I could feel my face getting red. "It's not what you think!"

She grinned. "To answer your question, I guess I don't know. He's never said. Why?"

"You know my teacher, Ms. Allen?" Sara nodded. "Well, she's been acting different lately. Today she showed up in a red dress! And I think she went into Mr. Campbell's room after school!"

Sara's eyes got huge! "Wow! Why, that's better than any soap I saw all day today!"

"I'm not positive," I said.

"So who cares?" Sara said.

Suddenly, something popped into my head. I remembered that Christians aren't supposed to gossip! "So don't tell anyone, please!" I begged.

"I promise!" Sara said.

"Not to change the subject, but do you see anything different about me?" I asked.

"Your hair looks nice," she said. "And isn't that a new blouse?"

"Thanks for noticing!" I said. "It's getting late! I'd better be going."

"There's one more thing before you leave," she said. "We have to weigh ourselves! Otherwise we won't know how well we're doing on our diets!"

Sara led the way into the bathroom. She went first. Then she wrote down her weight on a piece of paper. "Now it's your turn, Katie!"

I stepped on the scales. We watched the red hand quiver to a stop.

"Try it again, Katie!" she said. "This time take off your shoes!"

Actually, it didn't make any difference. I still weighed almost ten pounds more than Sara! And all those awful fat feelings came back!

"Don't feel bad, Katie!" Sara said. "Just think of how much progress you'll be making!"

"Right!" I said, trying to sound confident. "I really do have to go home. Think you'll be in school tomorrow?"

"Maybe." She coughed. "If I'm not at the bus stop, will you pick up my assignments again?"

"Sure!" I grinned. "What are friends for?"

Well, Mom never did say anything about my new shirt. I bet she forgot she ever bought it! I couldn't help realizing how excited she is about the pink outfit she's making for Amy!

But Dad noticed! After supper he hugged me. "You sure look nice today, Valentine!"

"Thanks!" I said.

"You seem lots happier than last night!"

"I am!"

"Why don't you come and tell me about it?"

"I can't," I told him. "When I finish the dishes, I have to make something in the kitchen!"

"I love you, Katie!" he said, smiling.

"I love you too, Dad!"

The only Jell-O we had on hand was lime. Actually, I was tempted to put in a can of crushed pineapple, like Mom usually does. But I didn't. When I finished, I hid the bowl on the bottom shelf of the refrigerator, way in the back.

As I turned out the kitchen light, I realized I was smiling. I do feel lots happier! I even hummed to myself as I went up to my room.

"OK, this is it!" I told my dolls. "Don't faint! I'm cleaning up this mess!"

I Start
on My New Image

I woke up feeling fantastic! Turning on my light, I looked around my room and smiled. Not to brag, but it's as neat as my brother's! Who says people can't change! And sure, I thought, I might be a little on the heavy side. But that will change too! Starting today!

Later, as I shivered in front of my closet, January looked up and thumped his tail. "I've changed! I'm cool!" I told him. "Not just cold," I laughed, "but *cool!*"

Actually, I nearly froze to death while I tried to remember what the cool kids wear! Jeans? My new jumper? I had no idea. To be honest, I'm not even sure who the cool kids *are!* I'd never singled them out as being that special!

"I'm wearing the jumper!" I announced. My dog whined his approval. What Mom would say was another matter. The jumper is what I've been wearing to Sunday school.

Just to show how serious I am about this image thing, I even considered wearing pantyhose! I mean, I might as well change totally! But I ended up wearing tights. Then, believe it or not, I actually put the pantyhose back in my top drawer! Today, if Jason looks in my door, he'll faint!

I decided to try something different with my hair. But frankly, my hair has a mind of its own. A side part didn't work at all, and it was too late to think of something really radical—like curls! Which is why I ended up with a kind of ponytail.

I wasn't sure what would happen when I got downstairs for breakfast. Suddenly, all I could think of was that huge bowl of lime Jell-O!

"You look nice, Katie," Mom said, as she glanced up from feeding Amy. "But it looks like you could use some help with that ponytail!"

"I don't want help!" I told her. "I like it this way!"

"Suit yourself," she said. "There's brown sugar for the oatmeal."

I walked past the table and stood at the refrigerator. Carefully I removed the leftover macaroni and cheese from in front of my big bowl of

Jell-O. Had Mom seen it? I wondered if she was watching as I spooned the green glob into my empty dish.

Have you ever really taken a good look at Jell-O? It's shinier than I remembered! As I returned it to its hiding place, it trembled. Next I carried my cereal bowl over to the counter. I stood there, my back to Mom, and ate the first bite.

Actually, it tasted super! I smiled. I thought of Sara, at her house, eating her lemon Jell-O. Having a friend was cool! She was right! This diet thing was going to be fun!

I held the third bite in my mouth until it melted. I never remembered Jell-O was so sweet!

"Valentine's Day is coming up," Mom said. "I'm going down to the Springs today. Do you want me to pick up some valentines for you?"

"Please don't," I told her. "This year I'm going to get my own valentines."

"Suit yourself," she said. "I just thought I'd offer."

Now, as I took another bite, I studied the color of the stuff in my spoon. Suddenly, it looked incredibly green! Come on, Katie! It's no big deal! Lots of foods are green! Like peas. And beans. *But not this color green!* I thought. On the next bite I gagged!

I tried to get a hold of myself! Maybe if I

talked to Mom I would stop thinking about what I was eating. I was almost done! "What's in my lunch?" I asked.

"Your favorite!" she said. "Liver sausage! And I even put in a Hershey bar!"

"Do we have to talk about it now?" I asked. "Can't we ever talk about anything besides food?"

"You seem upset," Mom said.

"Well, I'm not!" I took a deep breath and gulped down the last of my Jell-O. Then I turned to Mom. "How come you keep thinking I'm upset? This started out to be such a good day, too!"

"Katie, these days I feel as if everything I say to you is wrong!"

I didn't reply. Inside, I was wondering how our relationship ever got so messed up! Do other mothers care so much? That's it! She has too much time to think about me! Mom wouldn't be on my case all the time if she had a job!

"Don't worry about me so much!" I told her. "I'm perfectly able to run my own life!"

"Suit yourself!" Mom said. "If you ever want a mother again, I'll be here!"

All the way to the bus stop I was hoping Sara would be there! But she wasn't! As I got close, I could see Calvin watching me.

"How about that Ms. Allen!" Calvin said. "She's some cool teacher!"

45

Christopher laughed. They both watched to see how I'd react.

"Forget it!" I told them. "She's not your type! Besides, in case you haven't noticed, Ms. Allen's too old for you!"

"Well, thanks for pointing that out!" Calvin said. "Now I know why I'm so attracted to you, Katie! You're so practical!" It didn't sound like a compliment.

We just stood there. Finally Calvin spoke up again. "Katie, are you OK?"

"Sure," I said. "Why?"

He laughed. "I just noticed something. Your hat has a big bump in it!"

Now, as I rode the bus alone again, I missed Sara more than ever! What if the kids thought I looked dumb? Maybe they'd think I was going to Sunday school or something! Maybe Mom was right about my ponytail! Suddenly, I wished I could go back to bed and begin the whole day all over again!

Well, I needn't have worried. No one even said a word! I guess that's how it is. Actually, I realized that most people never give out compliments! All I know is that I'd have given anything to have someone say they liked my jumper. But no one did!

Today, school was incredibly boring. Ms. Allen, back in her navy blue jacket, stopped attract-

46

ing attention. The most exciting thing that happened all morning was when my stomach growled!

I wondered what Sara would say when she heard I hadn't eaten Jell-O for lunch. But no matter what she thought, it just wasn't possible.

"New dress?" Kimberly Harris caught up with me on the way to the lunchroom.

I beamed. "My mom made it for me for Christmas," I told her.

"You're lucky," she said. "My mother and I had to drive all the way to Denver to get me one."

"Is Denver cool?"

"It's OK," Kimberly said. "No offense, but I still prefer shopping in Philadelphia."

"That figures!" I laughed. She doesn't talk about her old home nearly as much as she used to! We sat down together.

Then I had an idea. "Want to trade that yogurt for a liver sausage sandwich?" I asked.

She shook her head. "And a Hershey bar?" I added.

"No way!" she said. "Too fattening!"

I watched the tall, thin girl. I've never said this to anybody, but Kimberly Harris looks exactly like a yardstick! "I thought you were trying to gain weight!" I said.

"Not anymore!" Kimberly pulled out a *Vogue* magazine. "Katie, just look at these models!"

47

I thumbed through several pages. Every picture looked like Concentration Camp Weekly! "Frankly, they all look like they're starving!" I said.

She ignored my comment. "Notice the clothes! And the beautiful houses! And take a look at all those men flocking around! It looks pretty cool to me!"

"I'm surprised, Kimberly," I told her. "I always thought you were more into improving your mind!"

She laughed. "Katie, get real!"

My stomach growled again. I decided to skip my sandwich. But I did eat the Hershey bar. After all, I had a whole afternoon of classes ahead of me. I had to do something to keep my energy up!

Hair Today, Gone Tomorrow

When I got to Sara's, I couldn't believe my eyes. She was sitting on the couch with a towel wrapped around her head like a turban.

"Wet hair!" I said. "Aren't you cold?"

"Nope. This house is like an oven!" She grinned. "Don't worry! I'm better! Actually, I probably could have gone to school today!"

"Well, I brought your assignments anyway," I said. "I'm glad you're OK. I've missed you!"

"Me too," she said. "Today I got so bored that I actually turned off the TV! Then I took a whole new look at my life! Katie, I can hardly wait to tell you my plan!"

"Don't tell me you decided to *gain* weight!"

Sara ignored me. "Katie, just listen to this! I'm

changing my image! From now on, Sara Wilcox is going to be cool!"

I didn't know what to say. If I told her I decided the same thing, she'd think I was just copying her! "Just how are you going to manage that?" I asked.

She smiled. "Well, the diet is the first step! Isn't it exciting! I feel thinner already!"

"Me too," I said. "How's the lemon Jell-O?"

"The best!" She grinned. "What flavor are you eating?"

"Lime," I told her. "It's the best too!"

"Maybe I'll have lime next!"

I hadn't thought of that. "How long do you think we'll have to keep dieting?" I asked.

Sara rolled her eyes. "As long as it takes," she said. She sounded kind of mysterious.

"Sara, to be honest, I didn't actually eat Jell-O for lunch," I admitted. "I couldn't figure out how to take it to school."

Sara shook her head. "That's no good, Katie! For a diet to work, you need commitment!"

"That's easy for you to say!" I told her. "You were here at home all day! And you never eat dinner with your mother anyway!"

"There's always a way!" Sara said. "Personally, I'm taking my Jell-O to school tomorrow in a thermos!"

"I don't think we have one."

"Then how about a glass jar?" Sara said.

"I guess that would work," I said. "But I still have to get out of eating dinner tonight!"

"You'll think of something!" she said.

I wasn't so sure. "What else are you going to do, Sara? Besides dieting, I mean."

"Next I'm planning to change my hair!" She grinned. "I think I'll become a blond!"

I giggled. "That would be a change all right!"

"Katie, I have an idea! We could do it together! You could become a redhead!"

"That's ridiculous!" I told her. "If being a red-head's so cool, how come you're changing? Your hair's not so bad."

She just looked at me. "Katie, I think you're on to something! Be honest, now. Do you really like my hair?"

She asked for it! I took a deep breath. "Well, sometimes it sticks up funny," I told her.

"It's that bad?"

"Not really bad," I said. "Maybe if you just trimmed off the parts that stick out!"

"Great! You can help me!" she said. "I'll get a pair of scissors!"

Actually, Sara's biggest worry was that we'd get hair on the carpet! Once we spread a sheet down, she relaxed. Then, after removing the towel from her head, she ran her fingers through the damp red curls.

I stood there holding the scissors. Carefully, I snipped off a piece that stuck out on the left. Now the right side seemed to stick out even farther. "Can you flatten your hair down with a brush?" I asked. "It's hard to tell what I've already cut!"

"I'll try," she said. She brushed away. But it was useless.

"I can't believe how your curls spring back!" I told her. "I hope they all end up the same length!"

"That's why I can't do it myself," she said. "Maybe while you cut, I could hold up a ruler!"

While Sara held a ruler out from her head, I tried to measure a curl and cut it before the hair snapped back into place. Suddenly, I started to laugh. "This is a riot! I hope nobody's looking!"

After ten minutes, Sara looked exactly the same! Only the piles of hair on the sheet showed how much I had cut off!

Sara studied herself in the mirror. "Katie, you did great!" she said. "Now it doesn't stick out anymore!"

I smiled. "Maybe I'll become a hair stylist!"

She smiled back. "Now it's your turn!" she said.

I just looked at her. "I already have a new ponytail," I told her. "Didn't you notice?"

"Mostly I noticed all that extra hair flying

around! And did you know your rubber band is almost falling off?"

"If I keep trying, I'll get better at it!"

"I don't know," Sara said. "Actually, I think you'd look very nice in bangs!"

"Maybe," I said. "Or I was thinking I might try to curl it!"

"It's your life!" Sara said. "But I'd bet anything your hair won't stay curly! And then you'll end up look exactly the same as you do now! Forever!"

"You may be right," I said. "Do you think you could do bangs?"

"Trust me!" Sara said.

We discovered that my hair is very different from Sara's! I mean, it's more than the color. My hair doesn't spring back. It just lies there.

While Sara worked, I had to keep my eyes closed. "How are you coming?" I asked.

"Fine!" she said. "I'm cutting them kind of long. Long bangs are very sexy!"

"I don't want to look sexy!" I said. "I want to see!"

Afterwards, I was afraid to open my eyes. I finally did, and Sara held up the mirror. I smiled. Although the edge of the bangs was kind of crooked, frankly, I looked real cool! "Wow! It looks like I've got a new image too!"

Sara kept looking at me. "Katie, is it just my

imagination, or do the bangs go downhill?" she asked. "Doesn't this side look higher?"

"It's OK," I told her. "I think it's just because the bangs don't lie down like the rest of my hair."

She put one hand on the top of my head and began to snip. "Hold still!"

"Oh, no!" I yelled. "You wrecked it! Now the other side is higher!"

"No problem! I'll fix it!"

"No you won't!" I said. "If you have your way, I'll be bald!"

"It isn't too noticeable!" Sara said. "Actually, I think you look really cool!"

I grinned. "Thanks! Let's clean up this mess. I have to go home."

"See you tomorrow!" Sara rolled her eyes. "We'll wow them together!"

All the way home, I tried to think of a plan to get out of dinner. I couldn't even let myself think of what Mom would say about my hair!

I hung up my jacket. But then I got an idea! I decided I'd just keep my knit hat on!

Mom noticed right away. "Katie, how come you're wearing that hat in the house?"

I faked a cough. "Mom, I think I'm catching Sara's cold." I blew my nose. "Actually, maybe it would be a lot better if I didn't eat with the family tonight."

"I'll take your temperature," Mom said. "Get the thermometer."

When I returned, my head felt all sweaty inside that stupid hat! I just knew I really would have a fever!

But when Mom held the thermometer up and looked at it, she said, "Perfectly normal!" She smiled. "Katie, you'd better plan to eat with us. We're having pot roast!"

"Mom, I can't!" I said. "Frankly, I wasn't going to mention it yet, but I can't eat with the family. I have to eat something special!"

"What are you talking about?"

I took a big breath and thought fast. "I have to eat Jell-O! Sara and I are trying out the world-famous Jell-O Diet! You've probably heard about it yourself!" I watched Mom's face. "Don't worry!" I told her. "It's already fixed and in the refrigerator!"

"I see," Mom said.

"Then it's OK?"

Mom shook her head. "You know the rules, Katie! Your father and I will expect you to eat with the family. As usual!"

Still wearing that dumb knit cap, I nodded. She was right. All my life, that's been our rule! I finished setting the table and rushed upstairs to wait in my room.

I Spill the Beans

Up in my room, I pulled off my hat. My hair was sopping wet! I thought about washing it and wrapping my head in a towel like Sara did. But I didn't think that would fly. So my only choice was to keep wearing the hat!

When Mom called, I started downstairs. I tried to ignore the red hat pulled down over my ears. Smiling, I pretended nothing was different!

As I joined the family around the table, Dad and Jason gave me funny looks. I closed my eyes. With luck, maybe they'd think I was praying!

"Praise God, from whom all blessings flow!" As the others began to sing, I joined in. Afterwards, I sat down and stared at my plate. Amy took one look at me from her high chair and laughed out loud.

"Hey, what's with the hat?" Jason asked.

I sighed. "You wouldn't understand," I said, trying to sound mysterious.

Dad grinned. "Is it a new style, Katie?"

I smiled at him. "Do you like it?" I asked.

Mom got impatient. "Steve, please pass the food! Everything's getting cold."

I didn't take any potatoes or carrots. I even let the pot roast sail right by.

"Not hungry?" Dad asked.

I glanced at Mom. I decided against using the word *diet*. "Actually, I'm eating something special tonight," I told him.

"Something light!" Jason said. "So light it's invisible!"

I took a deep breath. It was now or never. "May I please be excused for a minute?"

My parents looked at each other. "Just for a minute," Dad said.

I carried my plate over to the refrigerator. My bowl of green Jell-O was now stuck even farther in the back. It took forever until I returned to the table. As I sat down with my plate full of Jell-O, nobody said a word.

"More gravy, Jason?" Mom asked.

"Thanks, Mom! This is awesome!"

"I agree!" Dad said. "Elizabeth, you've outdone yourself this time!"

Slowly I filled my spoon with green Jell-O and took a bite. I couldn't believe it! Somehow, during the day, it had gotten even sweeter! I had to make myself take another bite.

"Has anybody seen our box of photographs since we moved?" Mom asked. "Upjohns are having a Valentine party, and everybody is supposed to bring their wedding pictures. Since we eloped, we don't have an album. But I do want to take that one framed snapshot we have."

No one was looking at me. "Not me! I haven't seen it," I said.

"Maybe the pictures are in that stuff we piled into our closet," Dad said.

Mom shook her head and sighed. "Then Heaven help us!"

My ears began to itch. I reached up under my cap and scratched them. And then I nearly choked on another bite of Jell-O. Frankly, it was getting harder and harder to pretend nothing was happening!

Suddenly, Mom took a good look at me and began to laugh! She has this incredible laugh. It's so contagious that everybody else just has to join in. Within seconds the whole family was cracking up! Including me!

"What's with the Jell-O?" Dad asked.

"It's not supposed to be funny!" I told them, trying my best to stop laughing. "Sara and I are on a Jell-O diet. To be honest, she was the one who heard about it first!"

"That figures," Jason said.

"But lime Jell-O!" Mom couldn't believe it.

"It doesn't have to be lime," I explained. "Actually, Sara's Jell-O is lemon!" Well, that made everyone laugh even harder!

I felt very relieved. "I wasn't going to spread this around, so don't tell anyone," I said. "Sara and I have decided to look cool!"

"Cool!" Dad laughed. "You should see your face, Katie! You look more like you're burning up!"

"And exactly how long have knit caps been cool?" Mom asked.

"They aren't," my brother said. "At least not in eighth grade!"

"The cap is only temporary," I explained. "It's only until I can wash my hair."

Mom's pretty sharp. She caught on right away. "You have a new hairdo?"

"Not exactly," I said slowly. "Can't we talk about this later?"

"Katie, are you sure you don't want any pot roast?" Dad asked.

"Well, maybe just a little. And just one potato. And two carrots."

I have a feeling that Dad changed the Bible verse just for me! After dinner, during family devotions, he read about being pretty *inside!*

Your beauty should not come from outward adornment, such as braided hair and the wearing of gold jewelry and fine clothes. Instead, it should be that of your inner self, the unfading beauty of a gentle and quiet spirit, which is of great worth in God's sight.

(I Peter 3:3, 4)

Afterwards, Dad winked at me. "Katie, I'm going to help Jason with the dishes tonight," he said. "Why don't you just go ahead and wash your hair!" It was a miracle!

Later, when I emerged from the bathroom, Mom was standing right there. "Well, what do you know!" she said. "Bangs!"

I watched her face. "Do you like them?"

She smiled. "I really do! What do you think?"

"Actually, I think Sara cut them crooked," I said. "And they won't lie down flat!"

"I have an idea," Mom said. "There's a woman in our Sunday-school class who works in a beauty salon. If you were to call Laurie, I bet she could help you out!"

I actually hugged Mom! "Thanks!" I said. "I hope she can fix it tonight! I would hate to go to school like this!"

Laurie had a nice voice on the telephone. "Katie, is this an emergency?"

"I'm not exactly sure," I told her. I looked at Mom. "Is this an emergency?"

"Kind of," Mom said.

In half an hour we were at Laurie's house and she was assessing the damage. "Cutting bangs isn't as easy as it looks!" she said. "Fortunately, your friend cut them pretty long!"

"Are long bangs really more sexy?" I asked.

Laurie glanced at Mom. "Not necessarily," she said. "Don't you want the boys to see your beautiful eyes?"

I just looked at her. I couldn't believe it. "My eyes are pretty?"

"Not just pretty!" Laurie told me. "Your eyes are beautiful!"

Afterwards, I almost danced out to Purple Jeep! "I'm really glad you're my mother!" I said.

Mom started the motor. Then she looked over at me and smiled. "Katie, I think I figured out why we've been rubbing each other the wrong way! Maybe it's because we're so much alike!"

That surprised me. "Mom, did you ever want to change your image?"

"Lots of times!" she said. "Sometimes I still do! But I'm learning to accept myself the way I am. That's how the Lord loves us—just the way we are!"

I remembered something. "But what if He never gives me a boyfriend?"

"Then He'll give you something else!" Mom told me. "Isn't that what happened to Mayblossom McDuff?"

She's the author who bought the mountain cabin where we used to live. Since then, she's become a special friend of mine. I thought about how happy M. is up there writing books. "You're right!" I said. "M. wouldn't trade with anybody! Mayblossom loves her life!"

We rode along in the dark. As we passed Sara's house, I remembered one thing that's still bothering me. But I was too embarrassed to ask Mom if she thinks I'm fat!

The Day
Calvin Changed

The next morning I overslept. All my plans for looking awesome went right down the drain. Without even a thought about color coordination, I grabbed a sweater and jeans. It's very hard to look cool when you forget to set your alarm clock!

I rushed into the kitchen. Mom had her own mouth open wide as she tried to spoon cereal into Amy's mouth. She looked up and smiled. "Your hair looks nice, Katie! I wonder why we didn't try bangs long ago?"

"All I did was brush it," I said. "I didn't have time to wash it again."

"No cereal?" she asked. "Don't tell me you're eating Jell-O for breakfast!"

I nodded and pulled the bowl from the refrigerator. The Jell-O looked very cold. And very green.

Mom shook her head and grinned. "Well, Katie, at least it will slide down in a hurry!"

The good news was that it did slide right down. The bad news was that I was still able to taste it! I shuddered. "OK if I take this glass jar to school?" I asked.

"Science experiment?"

"It's for my lunch," I explained. "I won't be needing a sandwich today."

Mom got the point. But she couldn't believe it. "Aren't you getting sick of it?"

"No way!" I lied. I emptied the last of the Jell-O into the jar. "But I think maybe I'll try strawberry next."

Sara was waiting at the bus stop near Calvin and Christopher. The first thing I noticed was her thermos. She hadn't forgotten! We were still in this diet together.

As I arrived, Calvin began to sing. "Here she comes! Miss America!"

"Don't be a jerk!" I told him. Although my ears were cold, everybody could see my hair! Actually, my red knit cap was wound around my glass jar! "So how are you feeling?" I asked Sara.

"Cool," she said, smiling. "Really cool." Her voice still sounded hoarse.

"Hey, Katie! I like your hair!" Christopher said.

I grinned. "Thanks!" I was starting to feel awesome.

"Well, I'm the one who cut it!" Sara bragged. "And Katie cut mine! How do you like it?"

"It looks just the same," Calvin told her. "It still looks just as red!"

"I was thinking of becoming a blond!" she told him. "Would that be more glamorous?"

Both boys began to laugh. And then Calvin let out one of his monster belches.

Sara giggled. "Don't tell me! I finally got to hear Calvin Young's famous belch!"

"It's famous?" Calvin asked. He did it again. This time was even louder.

"Nobody in our room even laughs anymore," I said. "We think it's crude!"

"Well, I think it's hilarious!" Sara couldn't stop giggling.

"You do?" Calvin smiled at her. "And where have you been all my life, Princess?"

Sara smiled a shy little smile. "I guess I've been waiting around for my prince!"

Calvin began to sing softly. "Some day my prince will come! Some day I'll find my love, and how thrilling that moment will be!"

"Cheap thrill!" I said. "Here comes the bus!"

Even after we sat down, Sara was still wired.

"Katie," she whispered. "He's starting to like me!"

"Who? Calvin?"

"Right!" She never stopped smiling.

"He just needs attention," I explained. "Actually, everybody in my room thinks Calvin Young is hopelessly immature!"

"I think Calvin needs to be appreciated," Sara said. "Everybody does."

"You just want a boyfriend!" I said.

"So what if I do?"

"But Calvin Young?" I couldn't believe it.

"Why not?" she asked. "You told me yourself that he isn't your boyfriend! Right?"

"Right!"

"Well, then why should you care?"

I didn't exactly know. So I decided to change the subject. "I have my Jell-O in this jar," I told her.

"Good!" she said. "I have an idea. Right after school let's weigh ourselves!"

As we got off the bus, I just happened to glance over at the parking lot. "Look!" I said. "Isn't that Mr. Campbell?"

"He's helping someone out of his car!" Sara said. "She's wearing a blue leather coat!"

"I can't believe it!" I said. "It's Ms. Allen!"

"You were right, Katie! It looks like I'm not the only one getting a boyfriend!"

67

"Sara, don't stare!" I said. "Keep walking. Pretend to be talking to me! Act cool!"

As she turned around, Sara nearly dropped her books. By the time we got organized again, the teachers had disappeared.

"This really is better than a soap!" Sara said.

When I got into my homeroom, Ms. Allen was already standing beside her desk. She was wearing the pink blouse and pearls again. She reminded me of a marshmallow—all soft and pretty.

"Katie! You look different!" Kimberly said. "You have bangs!"

I grinned. "Thanks!" I was glad someone noticed. To be honest, it is hard to keep feeling cool when nobody says a word!

"I like them!" said Michelle Davis, who sits across from us. "Katie, you really look cool!"

I couldn't believe it! This was turning out to be the best day of my life!

Then, during social studies, something else happened. First, I felt a poke in my back. When Ms. Allen wasn't looking, Robert Jackson handed me a note.

Now I felt even cooler! Actually, the truth is, I don't get a lot of notes! As a matter of fact, I probably haven't gotten one for at least two years! Smiling to myself, I slowly unfolded the piece of paper.

*Katie! What is Sara Wilcox's
telephone number?
Signed,
C. Y.*

I couldn't believe it! Don't tell me Sara was right! Was Calvin Young really starting to like Sara Wilcox? I suppose I should have been glad. But to be honest, I wasn't too thrilled. As I glanced around, I saw Calvin watching me.

Suddenly, it was as if I were seeing Calvin Young for the very first time! I couldn't believe it. Somehow he had changed! Now he looked fabulous! His eyes sparkled. And he had this cute, mischievous grin on his face. He saw me looking and winked.

Because I was afraid Ms. Allen would catch me, I didn't send the note back. I refolded the piece of paper and stuck it in my spelling book. I'd deal with it later.

At lunchtime, I knew I was in trouble as soon as I reached into my locker. My glass jar was warm. You guessed it! The Jell-O had melted.

"What's that, Katie?" asked Jennifer Thomas.

"It's a secret potion!" I told her. "It's going to turn me into a princess!"

"Or a frog!" said Sue Capelleti. "Are you really going to drink that disgusting stuff?"

"Sure!" I said, grinning. "Down the hatch!"

How was I to know it would spill? Actually,

everybody helped me clean up the mess. After we used up all the napkins, Kimberly ran to get paper towels from the bathroom. Mr. Hobbs, the principal, gave her a Golden Chance Award for being so thoughtful!

After school, I slipped Calvin's note back to him. But I decided not to tell Sara I had given him her telephone number. There was no use getting her hopes up. He probably wouldn't call anyway.

Sara and I headed right over to her house to weigh ourselves. She went first. "All right!" she hollered. "I lost a pound!"

I stood on the scale and we both looked down. "It isn't fair!" I said. In spite of all that green Jell-O, I now weighed a pound more than I did when I started!

Someone's Following Me

Sara and I didn't actually talk about our diet. But I think we both knew that once I stepped off that scale, I'd stop eating Jell-O!

Since she had to catch up on homework, I headed for my house.

Mom wasn't there. Instead, she had left a note on the kitchen table.

> *Dear Katie,*
> *Dad and I have taken Amy to the doctor. She's running a temp. Please start dinner. There's ground beef thawed.*
>
> > *Love,*
> > *Mom*

The first thing I did was change out of the sweater and jeans, which still looked kind of green from the Jell-O. To be honest, I was feeling pretty down. Nothing seemed to be working out like I thought it would.

Because I didn't want to think about Amy, I opened the refrigerator. Actually, it turned out to be a very large package of ground beef. And that gave me an idea. If I started now, I could make a meat loaf! And baked potatoes! Suddenly, my stomach growled and my mouth began to water.

I don't even need a recipe to make meat loaf! I broke an egg into a bowl, stirred it with a fork, and poured in some milk. Next, I added a teaspoon of salt and enough bread crumbs to turn it into mush. Finally, I cut up an onion and stuck that in. Last, I mixed in the ground beef. I patted the mixture into a loaf pan and stuck it in the oven.

The baked potatoes were easier still! After sticking each one with a fork, I inserted a nail. That's a trick Mom learned from her mother! What happens is this: the nails get hot, and that helps bake the center of the potatoes!

As I helped myself to an apple, I had another brainstorm! I could bake apples! That would give us a nice dessert! And everything would bake at the same time!

After cutting out the cores, I arranged the apples in a pan of water. Into the center of each apple, I put cinnamon, sugar, raisins, and a small piece of butter.

As I turned on the oven, I smiled. I could hardly wait for dinner! Wouldn't my family be surprised!

"January!" I called. The dog came running. I squatted down and gave him more loving than he's gotten for weeks. "We've got a good hour before this is done! Would you like to go for a walk?" He wagged his tail.

We headed out. This time we avoided the front road and cut through the land in back of Home Sweet Home. In no time we were in the country. Because I hadn't taken time to do much exploring, I didn't realize that my house is so near the edge of Woodland Park! Why, this was almost as private as the land near our cabin!

January and I ran until I got tired. And then we walked, taking time to look at an old barn desperately in need of paint. Although I didn't go inside, I decided it might be worth exploring another time.

And then we ran some more. January was having fun too. He'd dash ahead, then come back to me and wag his tail and grin.

"Hey, January, isn't this fun!" I said. "We'll have to do this again!"

Now it was getting dark. I was just about to turn for home anyway when I noticed a man coming toward me. January began to growl.

"Come on, January!" I said. "Let's get going!" I ran as fast as I could go.

But I didn't realize I had come so far! Before I reached the old barn, I was exhausted. And the man was catching up to us. He was running now. I could hear his feet pound behind me.

Suddenly, I was afraid. My chest hurt. I had slowed down so much that now I was hardly moving. And I couldn't keep running.

"Come on, January!" I grabbed the dog's collar and pulled him off to the side of the road. "I'm counting on you to protect me!" Until now it had always seemed dumb that Mom wouldn't let me go hiking all alone.

Immediately, January's nose went up in the air, and he began to howl. *AaaaaOoooooo!* It's what we call his "Star Spangled Banner" routine! To be honest, mostly it's been pretty embarrassing. But now it sounded like music to my ears!

AaaaaOoooooo!

The man was slowing down.

AaaaaOoooooo!

Now he stood in the shadows a few feet away. But I couldn't look at him. Frankly, I couldn't move. I was even too scared to talk.

"Don't be afraid! I won't hurt you!" said a voice. Actually, it sounded kind of familiar.

AaaaaaOooooo!

I opened my mouth and tried to talk, but nothing came out.

"I'm not chasing you," the voice said. "I was just jogging!"

Actually, it sounded just like Christopher Bean!

AaaaaaOoooooo!

"That's enough, January!" I told him. "I'm sure he gets the point!"

"Don't tell me it's Katie!" the voice said. "Not Katie Hooper!"

"Christopher Bean?" I asked.

He started laughing. "Right! I jog here almost every afternoon! I've never seen you out here before!"

"Wow! That's a relief!" I told him. "I'll be honest! You really scared me for a minute! You're so tall, I thought you were a man!"

"How about calling off that animal?"

"I'll try. But I can't always make January stop," I admitted.

I patted him and talked quietly. "It's OK, January," I said. "He won't hurt me. It's a friend from school."

AaaaaaOooooo!

"Where did he learn to howl like that?" Christopher asked. "I've never heard anything like it!"

"I think he made it up!" I said.

"Katie, I need to head home!" Christopher said. "Would you like to run with me?"

I had gotten my breath back while we talked. "Sure," I said. I held January's collar until Christopher got close.

"It's OK, fellow!" Christopher told the dog. All at once, January relaxed. His tail began to wag and he smiled at Christopher!

Christopher laughed. "If I didn't know better, I'd think the dog was smiling at me!"

"You don't know January!" I said. "He is smiling! It's one of the things he does best!"

Christopher smiled. "Come on! Let's go!" He began to jog.

January and I joined him. Actually, Christopher didn't run too fast. But before long I became winded again. It was embarrassing.

Now Christopher slowed down to a walk. "It takes time to build up your endurance," he said. "I've been doing this for weeks now."

"Maybe I could learn," I said. "Who taught you how to do it?"

Christopher laughed. "Nobody taught me! I just started running. I figured it was something I could do without an ocean nearby!"

"Do you miss California?" I asked.

"I sure do!" he said. "I'm really enjoying learning to ski, but it still isn't surfing!"

"Sometimes I wonder if I'll ever get enough money to buy skis!" I told him.

"Don't ever give up on your dream, Katie!" he told me. "Dreams are important! But I've found that sometimes you need something to do in the meantime!"

I smiled. "I think I'm ready to run again."

He smiled too. "Then let's go!"

January seemed to know I was all right. He ran ahead, stopping occasionally to look back at us. That's exactly what he used to do when I hiked with him up in Divide.

But naturally I got tired again. Christopher didn't seem to mind. "I like your dog!"

"Me too. Sometimes I feel bad because people think he's stupid!"

"Why do they think that?" he asked.

I laughed. "To be honest, January really isn't too smart!"

"I don't know!" he said. "Maybe they just don't give out awards for the things he's good at!"

I thought about what he said. "That's nice!" I told him.

For a minute Christopher didn't say anything. Then he smiled at me. "You're nice too, Katie!" he said. "I've lived all over the country, and I've never met a nicer girl than you!"

I didn't know what to say. It might sound dumb, but all I could think of was "Thank you!"

"Here's where I turn off," he said. "Maybe we could jog together again sometime."

"Maybe we could!" I smiled as I watched him go. And as I ran home, I felt as if my feet weren't even touching the ground!

Life Gets More Complicated

Suddenly, I remembered the meat loaf! Oh, no! Could it have burned? Just when I was starting to feel so responsible!

But when I rushed in, the house smelled wonderful! Grabbing two potholders, I pulled the baked apples from the oven. Next, I turned down the temperature so the meat loaf and potatoes would stay warm. And only then did I take off my jacket!

"Katie! What a lovely surprise!" Mom said, when she got home.

"I fixed meat loaf," I told her. Then I remembered something. "How's Amy?"

"She'll be fine, but she did need a shot!" Mom said. "Dad's bringing her in."

"Something smells out of this world!" Dad said, as he passed through carrying the sleeping baby.

"Katie fixed supper," Mom said. "Meat loaf and baked potatoes. And she even baked apples!"

"My favorite!" Dad said. I laughed. He says that about nearly everything.

"We still need a vegetable," I realized.

"How about green beans?" Mom pulled out a package from the freezer. "I'll fix them, Katie. You look like you need a break!"

I grinned. "While the dinner baked, I took January for a walk."

"It must have been some walk!" Mom smiled.

"I'll just wash up, and then I'll be right back." I felt all tingly inside.

My dinner was a super success! Even Jason said so. "No Jell-O tonight?" he asked, grinning.

"I may never eat Jell-O again!" I said. "Besides, the stupid diet didn't work. I actually gained weight!"

"Most fad diets don't work," Mom said. "And even if you do lose weight, unless you change your eating habits, you gain it right back again afterwards."

Dad smiled at me. "You look fine to me, Katie! You don't need to diet!"

"Are you sure?" I asked. I hesitated. "Sara thinks I'm plump!"

Everybody laughed. "A strong wind would blow that girl right away!" Mom said.

"In our family, we all eat the same food," I said. "How come you and Jason stay so thin? And Dad and I get plump?"

"Who, me? Plump!" Dad pretended to be hurt.

"No offense," I told him. "But, Dad, you are kind of large!"

"Different genes!" he said. "God made each person different. Our bodies need to store fat somewhere. Body fat isn't a disease!"

"We studied nutrition in school," Jason said. "How people feel about weight is picked up through television and advertising. In our country, the diet industry is big business!"

"Sara does watch a lot of TV," I said. "You mean thin people really aren't the happiest?"

Everyone laughed. "You don't have to wait to be thin to be happy!" Dad said. "Anyone can be happy right now!"

Actually, the happiest person I know is my father! But I didn't think of that when I was at Sara's.

"But some people really are too fat," I said.

"That's different," Mom said. "Obesity is a danger to health. People who really have weight problems should be under a doctor's care. Most of us just need to learn to eat moderate amounts of well-balanced meals."

"More meat loaf, Katie?" Dad asked.

I grinned. "No thanks! After that discussion, one helping is just perfect!"

"Nobody mentioned exercise!" Jason remembered. "Some people overdo that, too!"

"Guess what?" I asked. "I tried jogging this afternoon! January and I ran back behind Home Sweet Home. There are so few houses that it's kind of like being at the cabin."

Mom smiled. "It must have been good exercise. When I got home, you looked all sparkly and full of life!"

"I did?" It's funny, but that's exactly how I felt!

When I got to my room, for some reason I couldn't study. To be honest, I couldn't stop thinking about Christopher Bean!

Ever since Christopher entered our school last fall, all the girls in my room have been after him. For weeks, he was the main topic of conversation every day at lunch.

Even Kimberly Harris, who was also new, tried to get Christopher to pay attention to her. I watched her! But after that time when the three of us were together on the field trip, he never talked to her again.

Actually, come to think of it, Christopher never talks to any of the girls! They all want him for a boyfriend! But maybe all he wants is to be a plain old friend!

That's it! I thought. That's what Christopher seemed like today—a plain old friend. A friend who just happened to be a boy! Well, that suits me fine! Because personally, I wouldn't know what to do with a boyfriend anyway!

I smiled. My first real friend was Sara Wilcox. Is it possible that Christopher Bean might be my second?

Just when I was really into finishing my social studies, I got a phone call. It was Sara. "You'll never guess what happened!"

I faked it. "You lost another pound?"

"No!" she said. "That's another story."

I smiled to myself. I wouldn't tell her I gave Calvin her phone number. It would be more fun for her if I'd act surprised! "Sara, don't tell me you got a babysitting job!"

"I'm still working on it!" she said.

"You finished all your homework!"

"Right! But that's not it either!" I could hear her giggle.

"Boy, I don't know!" I said. "Sara, why don't you just tell me!"

"You'll never guess who called!"

"I give up!"

"You know Christopher? Christopher Bean?"

"Yes," I said slowly.

"He called me!" Sara said. "Christopher Bean actually called me!"

84

"Really?"

"Really!" she said.

"So, what did he want?"

"What do you mean?" she said. "He didn't want anything!"

"He must have wanted something! Why did Christopher call you?" I asked again.

"Katie, that's what boys do!" Sara said. "Boys call girls on the telephone!"

"For no reason?"

"Don't act so innocent, Katie!" Sara said. "Personally, I think there is a reason. I think they call because they're too embarrassed to talk to us in person!"

"What makes you think Christopher is too embarrassed?" I asked.

"Think about it, Katie!" she said. "Does Christopher Bean ever talk at the bus stop?"

"Sometimes he does!" I said.

"Hardly ever!" she said. "Although maybe it's just because that loud mouth Calvin Young does all the talking!"

"I thought you liked Calvin!" I said. "This morning you wanted him to be your boyfriend!"

"Katie, Katie!" she said. "At that moment, Calvin seemed to be my best possibility!"

"That isn't very nice, Sara!" I said.

"You should talk!" she said. "Calvin Young's been saying nice things to you since kindergarten! And you just brush him off like a dead fly!"

"That's what I've always done!" I told her. "Calvin knows I don't mean it!"

"Katie, grow up!" she said. "The guy has feelings. We aren't in kindergarten now, you know!"

"I just wish life didn't have to get so complicated!" I said slowly.

"By the way, Katie, I'm off the Jell-O diet!" Sara said. "When Mom found out, she nearly had a fit! Hope you aren't mad!"

"It's OK," I said. "As a matter of fact, I'm off Jell-O myself!" I took a big breath. Frankly, I was relieved when my brother came in and wanted the phone. "I have to go, Sara. See you in the morning."

Without a word, I handed my brother the telephone and slowly climbed the stairs to my room.

Calvin Likes Sara (Not Me)

Even though I ate a regular breakfast, I beat Sara to the bus stop. Christopher wasn't there yet, but Calvin seemed glad to see me.

"Hi, Katie!" He smiled.

"Hi, Calvin." I didn't know whether to bring up the phone number or not.

"Thanks for giving me Sara's telephone number," he said.

"You're welcome." Now I couldn't think of another thing to say.

He seemed unusually shy. "You probably can't believe this," he said. "Katie, I've never called a girl on the phone before."

I smiled. "I never called a boy either."

He seemed relieved. "You know all the times

87

I've teased you about being in love?"

"Yes?"

"I really didn't mean it," he told me.

"That's what I figured," I said.

He drew a circle with his toe. "Katie, do you think Sara really likes me?"

"Sure," I said.

"I'm glad," he told me. "Because I think I really like her!"

And that's when Christopher Bean came on the scene. "Hi, Calvin! Hi, Katie!"

We both said hi. Now Calvin's voice was a lot louder. "There's new snow at Breckenridge," he announced.

"Good!" Christopher pounded him on the back. "Man, I hope you're up for a challenge! This weekend I'm going to knock your socks off!"

Now there was silence. Fortunately, just then Sara arrived. I'm afraid I stared. She was wearing pantyhose and shoes with little heels. "Hi, everybody!" she said.

All three of us said hi. Then there was this awkward pause. I guess nobody could think of anything to say!

Suddenly, I remembered what it was like when nobody commented about what I was wearing. "I like your shoes," I told her.

"Thanks," she said, smiling.

"Yeah, Sara! You look great!" Calvin said. He

grinned. "Kind of like a princess!"

"Right," Christopher said.

Now Sara really smiled.

But talking wasn't easy. Finally Calvin said, "Sara, I'm glad you aren't sick anymore."

"Me too." She gave him a big smile. "But it worked out OK. When it comes to bringing home books, Katie Hooper's the greatest!"

"It isn't fair!" Calvin pretended to pout. "When I was sick, you never brought mine!"

"You never asked me!" I teased.

"I have an idea!" Christopher said. "What if we both catch something this weekend! And then on Monday Katie can bring both of us our books!"

"In that case, I'll help her!" Sara said.

"Now I know I'll get sick!" Calvin smiled at Sara and pretended to cough. "Actually, I'm already sick just thinking about it!"

"What fakes!" I laughed.

Calvin let out a grandfather of a burp.

Sara cracked up. "You should be on Johnny Carson!" she told him.

But on the bus, Sara seemed anxious. "Do you think he likes me?" she asked.

"Who?" I asked.

"Why, Christopher, of course!" Sara said.

"He might," I told her.

"I've been thinking. I wonder if Mr. Campbell

would let me transfer into your homeroom?"

"I doubt it. Why?" I asked.

"You're lucky, Katie! You get to be in the same homeroom with Christopher."

"So what?"

"That's true!" Sara realized. "Why, there must be a lot of girls in your room who are after him! And just think! He called me!"

Actually, she was sickening! I began to feel sorry I even said anything about her shoes! "Sara," I said slowly, "I think Calvin Young is starting to like you."

"Oh, him!" Sara said.

"Don't put him down!" I said. "There's nothing wrong with Calvin Young! He's really a lot of fun! Having him in our room is riots!"

"Big deal!" Sara said.

"Yesterday you were all excited just thinking Calvin might like you!" I pointed out.

"That was yesterday."

"Then how come you encouraged him just now?" I asked.

"So Christopher would get jealous!"

I shook my head. "I'm glad I don't want a boy-friend," I said. "At least I don't have to be a fake!"

"You know what I think, Katie? I think *you're* just jealous!"

"Don't be ridiculous!" I just sat there.

Finally she spoke. "I suppose you'll be getting rich babysitting tonight?"

"It isn't just for the money!" I told her. "Actually, I can't wait to see Doris and David!"

"Mom has to work, but maybe I'll go somewhere special," Sara said.

"By yourself?"

"Not by myself!" she replied. "Mom would ground me for life. But maybe I'll have a date!"

"A date! You have to be kidding!"

"Actually, it's not a bad idea!" she said. "Maybe I could get Calvin to take me somewhere. Wouldn't that make Christopher jealous!"

"You'd do that?"

"All's fair in love and war!"

"You don't really believe that, do you?" I asked. She just smiled.

As we rode home on the bus after school, I had a good idea. "Sara, it's a beautiful day! Let's go running in back of my house!"

"Running?"

"I tried it yesterday," I said. "Actually, it was fun!"

"Sorry, Katie, but it sounds boring! Count me out!"

"OK, then I'll take January."

"It's your life!"

"Maybe you'll change your mind, when you

see I'm getting physically fit!" I told her.

"Personally, I'm going to watch TV," she said. "Don't forget, Katie, I've been sick!"

To be honest, by then I wasn't too thrilled about running either. But I wouldn't admit that to Sara. Suddenly, I remembered that Christopher just might be there! I grinned. If Sara knew that, she'd come! For sure! But I decided not to tell her. If she didn't want to be physically fit, it was OK with me!

"I'll call you tomorrow!" she said. "Maybe we can go shopping!"

"Maybe," I said. "See ya!"

As I walked in the door, Mom was talking on the phone. "Oh, here she comes now!" Mom said. "It's Mayblossom McDuff."

"Hi, M.!"

"Hi, Katie! I have to drive down to the Springs tomorrow. Want to come along?"

"Sure!" I grinned.

"How about going down for lunch?"

"Really?" I nearly jumped up and down.

M. laughed her tinkling little laugh. "I'll pick you up about eleven."

"Thanks a lot!" I said. "I'll be ready!"

"What's up?" Mom asked. When I told her, she smiled. "It sounds like fun!"

"Now I think I'll go running," I told her. "Frankly, I think January needs the exercise."

Mom smiled. "Be home before dark!"

This time January and I jogged all the way to the old barn. I only had to stop to rest once. To be honest, I wasn't running very fast. But I wasn't just walking either.

Now all I could think of was Christopher Bean. "I wonder if we'll see Christopher?" I asked out loud.

January just grinned at me.

"It's not what you think!" I explained.

January wagged his tail.

"It's just that it would be nice to have somebody to talk to."

January stared at me.

"I know I have you," I said. "But frankly, you aren't quite the same as a real person!"

All at once, January acted like he heard something. He looked all around. Could it be Christopher? But then nothing happened. The dumb dog was just tracking a bee!

"I'll race you to that tree!" I said. We ran right past the place where we saw Christopher yesterday. He wasn't there. Finally, I turned around and began to jog slowly. "Let's go, January," I said. "Mom said to be back before dark!"

Sara's Newest Bombshell

I wasn't sure if I wanted to eat pancakes on Saturday morning or not. Dad and Jason always fix them. Although I wasn't on a real diet, I had decided not to eat things that had lots of calories.

"Maybe you could just eat fewer of them," Mom suggested, as we went downstairs.

I smiled. Now why didn't I think of that! Later, when Dad asked, "Another one, Katie?" I was ready with my answer. "No thanks," I said. "But they certainly are delicious!"

Sara called as I was finishing the dishes. "When shall I pick you up?"

"For what?" I asked.

"I thought we were going shopping!"

"I didn't know it was definite," I told her. "Mayblossom McDuff invited me to go with her to lunch in Colorado Springs."

"Oh."

"I'm sorry," I told her. "I really wish you could come too."

"That's all right," Sara said. "Call me when you get back. I have something to tell you!"

"Tell me now," I said.

She didn't need to be urged. "Katie, you'll never believe who called me last night!"

"Christopher?" I guessed.

"No," she said. "Calvin Young! And guess what? We talked for an hour and twelve minutes!"

"About what?"

"Katie, you still don't get it, do you?" She seemed impatient with me.

"You must have talked about something," I said.

She laughed. "Who knows! The point is that Calvin Young likes me! Now I'm sure of it!"

"Well, are you glad, or not?" I asked.

"I love it!" she said. "All my life I've wanted to be special to somebody! And now I have a boyfriend! Katie, it's a dream come true!"

I was confused. "But I thought you liked Christopher!"

"Well, sure!" she laughed. "Who doesn't! But

you were right, Katie! Calvin is barrels of fun!"

I don't know what got into me, but I felt like I had to impress her. "I think Mayblossom may be taking me to lunch in Wimsey," I bragged. "That's her little red sports car! She bought it for herself on her fiftieth birthday."

"Wow!" Sara said. "I've never ridden in a sports car. I wonder if Calvin will drive a red sports car when he's old enough?"

Calvin! Calvin! Calvin! I could hardly stand it. "I doubt it!" I scoffed. "It'll be a hundred years before he can afford something like that! He'll probably have to be driven all over town in his mother's station wagon!"

At first, Sara didn't say anything. "Well, at least I know one thing. My diet's working!"

"Diet! I thought you said you quit!"

"I did," she said. "This is a new one! It's an ice cream diet. Frankly, it's ten times easier to eat ice cream than yellow Jell-O! And Mom doesn't keep track of the ice cream."

"But now you already have a boyfriend," I said. "Sara, if you don't eat right, I'm afraid you'll get sick!"

"There you go again acting jealous," Sara said. "Why should I quit when I'm ahead? Just when I lose two pounds, I get my first boyfriend. Tell me, does that sound like success or what?"

I didn't know what else to say. Suddenly, I

found myself bragging again. "I wouldn't be surprised if Mayblossom takes me to lunch at some special place. Maybe even the Broadmoor!"

"Really?" Sara asked. "You're so lucky, Katie Hooper! Your family does so much. I never get to do anything special!"

"You go to Sunday school with us!" I said.

"Big deal!"

"I thought you liked it!"

"I do. But let's put it this way. If Calvin asked me to go skiing, guess which I'd pick!"

"Did he ask you?"

"Not yet," she said. "But I think it's just a matter of time!"

"But you don't know how to ski!" I said.

"Calvin taught Christopher! I bet he'd love to show off by teaching me!" Sara said.

"But you don't have skis!"

"I wouldn't have to buy them!" Sara said. "I could use some of my money and rent them!"

"You'd do that?"

"Just watch me!" she said.

And that's how our dream collapsed. At least it collapsed for me. It's hard to share a dream when the other person poops out!

"Call me when you get home!" Sara said. "I want to hear all about the Broadmoor!"

As I cleaned my room, I tried to figure out where Sara's coming from. She's right about one thing. She never gets to do anything special! Although my family includes her sometimes, she and her mother never seem to have plans.

"How come I'm so fortunate?" I asked the Lord. "First Sara's father died, and then her grandmother. And she has no brothers or sisters. She's all alone. It doesn't seem fair!"

With most of my things already put away, cleaning my room is much easier! Usually I spend most of my time picking up stuff!

"Lord, do You love Sara as much as You love me?" I asked.

Actually, I know the answer. Jesus loves everybody the same. But I didn't feel satisfied.

"Lord, if You love Sara so much, please don't let her slip away from You!" I prayed. "Give her something special. And please forgive me for being jealous when I already have so much!"

As I put on my blue jumper, I smiled. M. hadn't seen my bangs. She'd love them! And what could be more cool than riding in a red sports car to lunch at the Broadmoor! I came pretty close to praying that somebody from my room would see me! But I didn't.

"You look nice," Mom told me.

I smiled. "You don't think I should have worn tights, do you?"

"The stockings look nice. I didn't realize this was such a big deal!"

"It's my first time at the Broadmoor," I said. "I've been hearing about it all my life."

"Wow! I didn't know that's where you're going," she said.

I just looked at her. Mayblossom hadn't actually said we were eating at the Broadmoor! As a matter of fact, she hadn't even promised she'd drive the red sports car! Maybe she'd arrive in the four-wheel drive! And we'd eat at McDonalds!

"What's wrong?" Mom asked.

"Nothing."

"It's a perfect day for a drive! Actually, come to think about it, I wouldn't mind going down to the Springs with you!"

My fantasy was disappearing before my very eyes. No offense. I mean, Mom's OK. But if my mother went along, she and M. would do all the talking! And I'd have to sit there like a bump on a log.

Mom continued. "On the other hand, I probably shouldn't take Amy out yet," she said. "And I can't leave her with your father. He has a deadline on a sketching project. And Jason's with his committee from the youth group."

"Too bad," I said.

Mom smiled. "It's OK. There'll be another time."

I stood at the window and watched for M. Suddenly, I saw Wimsey pull up! I could feel a smile spreading over my entire face. "She's here!" I said. "And she's driving Wimsey! I'll see you!"

I nearly slipped as I ran out in my good shoes. "Hi!" I yelled.

"What a day for a drive!" M. said. She smiled as I climbed into the other seat. "Katie! You look different! You have bangs! I love your hair!"

"Thanks!" I smiled so wide the corners of my mouth felt tight.

"I'm glad you're all dressed up!" she said. "As I was getting ready, I had the best idea! What if we have lunch at the Broadmoor?"

Lunch at the Broadmoor

I think I'll always remember that drive down to Colorado Springs. Actually, we hardly talked at all. Although once in a while she'd look at me and smile, Mayblossom concentrated on driving. And I didn't concentrate on anything. I just felt wonderful and enjoyed the feeling. Life seemed to stretch out ahead of me like the road—smooth and sunny.

As we rounded a curve, we were slowed down by a tractor crawling along ahead of us. M. was patient. In a few minutes her chance to pass came, and she waved as she went by. I smiled and waved too.

"Life is like that, Katie," Mayblossom said. "Sometimes there are obstacles in our path. But the Lord either takes them away or helps us get around them."

"There's always something, isn't there?" I asked.

"There's always something." She smiled. "But it never surprises the Lord!"

Colorado Springs is spread out at the bottom of the mountains. It's the biggest city I've ever seen. To be honest, I'm glad I don't live there! But if I did, I suppose I'd like it!

I grinned. "Sometimes life turns into a regular traffic jam!" I said.

"How true!" M. laughed. "And sometimes it seems like all you do is wait!"

Once we got lost when we missed a turnoff. But finally Mayblossom pulled up in front of a meat market. "Want to come in?" she asked.

"Sure."

"I'm ordering steaks for a party next week," she told me. "The singles at church are coming up to my cabin for a steak fry."

"That sounds cool!"

"It will be wonderful!" She smiled. "We're having a treasure hunt in the afternoon. And after supper, we're planning a sing-along in front of the fire. Did you know your friend Sam Johnson plays the guitar?"

"Silent Sam?"

"He has a beautiful voice," M. said. "Sometimes people who don't talk much are full of surprises!"

Although I'd never seen it, I guess everybody knows that the Broadmoor is a fancy hotel. I hadn't realized that it's pink. As we walked up the circular driveway, a row of flags flew straight out in the wind. I hoped the bells in the tower would chime, but they didn't.

As the doorman held open the door and we entered, I gasped. I didn't know any place could be that beautiful! "It's like Heaven!" I said.

M. smiled. "Not quite! I think we go this way, Katie," she said. "The place where we'll be eating is supposed to be a greenhouse."

As we entered the restaurant, it was like walking into a cave! Frankly, it was so dark I could hardly see a thing! I think there were people sitting at tables, but I'm not positive. And then, suddenly, my eyes were nearly blinded!

Mayblossom laughed. "I feel like Saul on the way to Damascus!" she said.

Once we sat down I glanced around. People were all dressed up. I was glad I wore my good shoes!

"Are you hungry?" M. asked. "What looks good?"

I tried to concentrate on the menu in front of me. So many choices! And most of the things I had never heard of! Should I fake it?

"Katie, have you ever tried quiche?" M. asked.

I shook my head. "What's that?"

"It's kind of like a custard pie with cheese and bacon in it. I think you'd like it."

I smiled. Trying something new was part of the fun. When I had lunch at Mayblossom's before Christmas, she had introduced me to mushrooms. "I'll try it!" I told her.

"I think I'll go with the fresh fruit!" M. said. "I usually eat a light lunch."

"I'm sick of Jell-O," I told her. "Sara and I just tried a Jell-O diet!"

M. laughed. "Really? Tell me about it."

"Well, I ate lime Jell-O, and Sara ate lemon Jell-O. Actually, I gained a pound and she lost one!"

"It doesn't seem fair, does it!" M. said.

"That's what I thought!" I said. "Especially since Sara already looks like a toothpick!"

Mayblossom gave the waiter our orders. I took a sip of water. The floating lemon slice nearly hit me in the nose!

"M., can I ask you something?" I took a deep breath. "Be honest. Do you think I'm plump?"

She didn't laugh. "No, I don't," she said. "Katie, young girls shouldn't be dieting! If you eat well-balanced meals and get the right exercise, your weight will take care of itself!"

I smiled. I was glad to hear her say that!

Maybe my family knows something after all!

"Now Sara's on an ice cream diet!" I said. "M., is it true that you can lose weight eating ice cream?"

"It sounds as if Sara could be heading for a bad problem!" Mayblossom said.

Just then the waiter brought our food. The quiche looked delicious. After we prayed, we started eating. Then I discovered that quiche tastes even better than it looks!

After we'd taken a couple of bites, M. picked up our conversation where we had left off. "Why is Sara so anxious about being thin?"

"I think it's because she wants a boyfriend," I said. "And it worked. Calvin Young likes her."

Mayblossom smiled. "I expect he would have liked her anyway! Sara is certainly full of pep!"

"Is that why boys like girls?"

M. laughed. "Boys like girls for all kinds of reasons! Tell me, why does Sara like Calvin?"

"Actually, I'm not sure that she does," I said slowly. "She can't seem to make up her mind. I think she just wants a boyfriend. She doesn't really care who he is!"

"Does Sara feel good about herself?"

"What do you mean?" I asked.

"Does Sara like being Sara?"

I shook my head slowly. "I don't think so. Sometimes I think she wishes she were in my family! Actually, M., her life isn't very special!"

"Oh, yes it is!" M. said. "Everybody's life is special! But sometimes people just can't see it! Does Sara know Jesus?"

"I'm not sure," I said. "I've told her about Him. Sometimes she prays. And she comes to Sunday school. But, to be honest, I don't think Jesus is the most important thing in Sara's life."

"That's a good place to start!" Mayblossom said. "When you realize how much Jesus loves you, it's a lot easier to love yourself!"

"Can I ask you something very personal?"

"Sure! Ask away!"

"Mayblossom, are you really happy?"

"Certainly!" She smiled. "Can't you tell?"

"Wouldn't you like to be married? Don't you ever get lonely?"

"Sure!" she told me. "But I don't have to have a man. I think the Lord is turning me into a pretty neat person. I have lots of interests and lots of friends. Sharing my joy with somebody would be nice, but I don't really *need* anyone else!"

"You must have felt awful when your boyfriend was killed in the war," I said.

"Of course I did at the time!" Mayblossom smiled. "But the Lord led me around that obstacle. And I've had a wonderful time getting to know Him! My life seems perfect, just as it is!"

I could see she meant it.

"I know one boy I like," I admitted. "But just as a friend. Frankly, I don't really understand boyfriends and girlfriends!"

Mayblossom reached over and patted my hand. "Katie, at your age, most boys would probably rather have a true friend!"

"Are you sure?" I asked.

"I'm positive!" She smiled.

We had finished eating, and M. gave the waiter the money to pay the check. As we stood up to leave, M. suggested we take a walk to see the lake and the ice skating.

As I was following her out, I felt someone touch my arm. "Katie," said a voice.

I stopped. It was Ms. Allen! Frankly, I nearly fainted. "I didn't expect to see you here!"

She smiled. "I saw you come in. I'd like to introduce you to my friend. Katie, this is Kevin McMann."

The man stood up and smiled. "Hi, Katie! Alicia has been telling me about you."

"Oh, oh!" I said. I felt really stupid. I didn't know what to say.

Ms. Allen's eyes sparkled. "Katie, can you keep a secret? I just have to tell someone! Kevin has just asked me to marry him!"

"No kidding! And what did you say?"

"She said yes!" Kevin told me. "I have a

diamond ring for her. But we've decided to wait and make it official on Valentine's Day!"

Ms. Allen couldn't stop smiling. "Can you keep the secret that long, Katie?"

"I promise I won't tell anyone," I said. "Not even Sara Wilcox!"

Ms. Allen turned to Kevin. "Sara's in Jim's class," she explained. Then she looked at me. "Mr. Campbell is Kevin's brother-in-law. He's the one who introduced us!"

"So that's it!" I said. Suddenly I remembered where I was. "I'd better go! Ms. Allen, I'm really happy for you!" As I turned away from her still-smiling face, I felt like skipping right out of the room!

Sara's First Romance

On the way home from church the next day, Mom had good news. "I'm ready to help you girls start making your quilts!"

"Can I really make one with stars on it?" Sara asked.

"I have the patterns all cut out," Mom said. "Stars for you, and hearts for Katie!"

"Are you sure I'll be able to do it?" Sara asked. "I've never done any sewing, you know!"

"I'm sure," Mom said. "Of course, it's going to take a lot of patience!"

Personally, I could hardly wait. When we first moved here, I had the yuckiest room you've ever seen. But my family had a painting party which turned the walls white. And then Mom stenciled hearts around the top. Hearts happen to be my symbol. Now the only thing missing is something nice to cover my bed.

As I walked to the bus stop Monday morning, I thought about Ms. Allen's secret and smiled. Naturally, I hadn't told anybody. Now I couldn't wait to see her!

Sara and Calvin were off to one side talking. Or, I should say, Calvin was talking. For once in her life Sara was actually listening.

"What's going on?" I asked Christopher.

"Calvin's telling her all about slaloms," he said. "He skied in a slalom race Saturday."

"Were you in it too?" I asked.

"Are you kidding! I'm not that good!" he said.

I watched Sara. She was hanging on every word. I had no idea she even cared.

Finally, they looked up and saw me. "Calvin's been telling me all about slalom racing," she said. "He's an expert!"

"Not really," he said with uncharacteristic modesty.

She punched him and smiled. He grabbed her cap and ran—with Sara chasing him. I couldn't believe it. That's so immature that kids stopped doing it in the first grade!

"The bus is coming," I told them.

When we sat down on the bus, Sara was all excited. "Isn't he cute!" she gushed.

111

"If you say so," I said. "Just when did you get so interested in slalom racing?"

"Frankly, I'm not," she said. "But I heard that boys like it when you're interested in what they do!"

"What if Calvin finds out you're just faking it?" I asked.

"He won't find out!" she said. "This performance will win me my first Academy Award!"

In homeroom, Ms. Allen looked positively beautiful! And I couldn't say a word! Actually, I was even afraid to look right at her in case we'd both start grinning and blow it!

At lunch the girls were still talking about her. "Want to hear something bad?" Sue asked. "I saw Ms. Allen talking and laughing with Mr. Campbell! And he's married, you know!"

My heart sank. "They probably were just discussing report cards or something," I said.

"Oh, sure!" Pam rolled her eyes. But then everybody started talking about report cards and making the Honor Roll.

After school I figured Sara would come home with me and we'd start our quilts! I could hardly wait.

"I can't do it today," she said. "Calvin and I are going downtown. Sorry!"

Mom was disappointed too. "Katie, do you want to go ahead and get started without her?"

"Not really," I said slowly. "It's so nice out. Maybe I'll just take January and run again."

"It's certainly putting a sparkle in your face, Katie!" she said.

Christopher wasn't there. But to be honest, I didn't even care! Today I realized that I love to run! I jogged all the way to the barn without stopping once. I think even January was impressed!

The next morning Calvin and Sara weren't talking much. They just stood and smiled at each other. It was sickening!

In homeroom the main thing was that we got our report cards. Although I hoped for better grades, mine was no surprise. I got my usual— mostly B's with a C- in penmanship. And as always, I promised myself to do better next time.

Ms. Allen is really getting into plans for our Valentine Party! I can understand why! I wonder if teachers ever count the days until something's going to happen?

Now the whole school knows that Calvin and Sara are an item! After lunch, he actually went over and talked to her instead of playing soccer!

"Aren't you gonna sit with your girlfriend?" yelled a fourth grader, as we climbed on the bus.

"Is that a dare, or what?" Calvin called.

"Chicken! Chicken! Chicken!"

Well, nobody calls Calvin Young a chicken

without getting punched! And that's how Calvin got in big trouble.

"Poor darling," Sara said. "And he did it for me! If that isn't true love..."

"It isn't," I said. "He just doesn't want to be called a chicken!"

"Katie! Katie!" she said. "You still don't understand, do you?"

Well, to be honest, I was getting pretty sick of that line! So when she asked if we were going to start our quilts, I said I was busy! Actually, I ended up running faster than I ever did before!

The next day, Calvin showed everybody! He actually sat next to Sara on the bus! I mean *nobody* does that! And the worst of it was that it left me sitting with a little boy in third grade! I didn't even ask his name!

When we got off the bus after school, I walked by myself right behind the two of them. Just when I thought life couldn't get much lower, Christopher caught up with me. "Well, it looks like we've both lost our best friends," he said, smiling.

I smiled too. But I couldn't think of anything to say. Finally I asked, "Are you still running?"

"Every day!" he said. "I've found a new place closer to my house. Have you ever tried it again?"

"I've been going almost every day too!" I told

him. "I discovered I really enjoy it!"

"No kidding!" he said. "I really didn't think you'd go for it! Nobody else around here has!"

"If I tell you something, don't laugh!"

"I won't," he said.

"It sounds stupid, but I *feel* so good when I do it!"

"Me too!" He smiled as we got to my house. "See you tomorrow."

I hung around the kitchen for a while waiting for Sara to phone. But she never did. "Come on, January!" I called. "Let's run!"

"Want to start your quilt today?" Mom asked on Thursday.

"Sara acts as if I'm not alive!" I said. "Even though we sat together this morning, all she talked about was Calvin!"

"It's hard, isn't it?" Mom smiled.

Well, at least my mother understands. She did some hand sewing while I cut out hearts from several different pieces of calico. But I'd be lying if I said I didn't miss Sara. I've gotten used to doing things with her, and being with Mom just isn't as much fun as it used to be!

But at the bus stop Friday morning, Sara stood alone. Calvin was way on the other side, talking with Christopher.

"I suppose you've heard?" Sara said.

"Heard what?"

"Calvin and I have broken up! His mother won't let him come over to my house."

"Your mother wouldn't like it either," I said. "Did she know?"

She shook her head. "Katie, I feel awful," she told me. "Actually, I think I feel worse than I did before! The kids at school will all laugh at me. And now I have nobody!"

"Sara, that's not true," I said. "You still have me!"

She seemed surprised. "After the way I treated you?"

"I forgive you, Sara," I told her. "I don't think you really meant to leave me out!" I smiled. "Hey, after school, do you want to go running with me?"

"Running? Katie, are you crazy?"

"Then how about asking Mom if she's free to help us with our quilts?" I said.

"Now you're talking!" Sara said, smiling. "By the way, Katie, do you know the name of that cute guy over there? The one in the orange earmuffs?"

The New
Sara Wilcox

I may not always be cool, but I'm not stupid. It looked to me like my relationship with Sara Wilcox was never going to be the same again! I'd spend the rest of my life having fun with her only whenever she didn't happen to have a boyfriend!

Since I already had my hearts cut out, I helped Sara cut out the stars for her quilt. Then, while I began to baste hems on the hearts, Mom started showing Sara how to sew. Frankly, it's a good thing she's patient, because Sara isn't. The afternoon would have been grim if it weren't for Mom's sense of humor.

"Let's try it once more." Mom giggled. "And, Sara, please try not to shake! Just aim the

thread right at that hole in the needle!"

"Why can't they make the holes bigger?" Sara asked. "I feel so clumsy!"

"Everybody does at first!" I told her. "You'll learn!"

But finally even Mom gave up. "We'll begin with the hemming next time, Sara! After all, threading the needle is a wonderful start!"

There was still a little time left in the afternoon. "Are you sure you don't want to jog?" I asked. "We could go just a little way."

Sara smiled. "I think I'll watch TV! That's something I'm very good at!"

"Want to go to the 5 and 10 tomorrow?" I asked. "I still don't have my valentines."

"Sure!" she said. "I'll call you."

But when Sara called Saturday morning, she had other news! "Katie! You'll never guess who called me!"

"Here we go again!" I said.

She laughed. "This time it wasn't a boy! It was Mayblossom McDuff! She called last night! And guess what! This afternoon she's taking me to lunch at the Broadmoor!"

I was speechless. I couldn't belive it.

"At last I'm going to get to ride in Whitney!" she said.

"You mean Wimsey?" I asked.

"The red sports car!"

"Wimsey," I told her. "It's named after a character in a book."

"Whatever! Sorry about the valentines, Katie," she said. "But I knew you'd understand! I'll call you as soon as I get home!"

"Right," I said. "Bye." And I heard her hang up the phone.

"What's wrong?" Mom asked.

"Mayblossom McDuff is taking Sara for lunch at the Broadmoor," I said.

Mom smiled. "How nice!"

I pretended to smile. "I'm going to get ready to go downtown," I said. "I have to get my valentines." I went up to my room and closed the door.

To be honest, I was totally unprepared for this! How could M. do it? I thought our special relationship would be saved for me alone! Tears filled my eyes. It wasn't fair! I felt angry and betrayed.

After a few minutes, a thought popped into my mind and wouldn't go away. I knew it had to be the Lord. *Katie, you prayed for something special for Sara, didn't you?*

"Sure," I prayed. "But Mayblossom is *my* special friend! I don't want to share her with somebody else—especially not Sara!"

You share other things!

"That's different!" I said.

But Sara needs someone!

120

"Give Sara somebody else!" I told Him.

I love Sara too, Katie!

Finally, I couldn't stand it any longer! I put on my jacket and left. Actually, I ended up running most of the way to the 5 and 10.

Reading the valentines didn't seem to help at all! The warm and loving words all seemed to mock me. And the funny ones seemed cruel.

"Hi, Katie! Getting your valentines?" It was Calvin Young.

"How come you aren't skiing?" I asked.

"We're going tomorrow. Are you here alone?" I nodded.

"I hope Sara isn't mad at me," he said. "What happened was nothing personal. I just realized that I'm not ready to have a real girlfriend."

I was surprised. "You aren't?"

"No," he said. "Maybe next year. Or the year after that. Or maybe not until I'm in high school!"

"I know what you mean," I said. "I'm not ready either! For a boyfriend, that is!"

He smiled. "As you've probably noticed, I'm all talk!" He laughed nervously. "And now it's too late for that! I sure messed up! I can't even tease you anymore, Katie Hooper!"

I smiled. "If you want to, you can!" I said. "Actually, Calvin, I think it's kind of fun!"

"Katie, you're so honest!" he said. "You know,

it's funny. I feel like I can really trust you! If I ever do get a girlfriend, I hope I find one as nice as you!"

"Thanks, Calvin!" I said. "You've made my day!"

He grinned. "Be still my heart!" he said.

Suddenly, after he left, I realized I felt incredible! I can't believe it! I have another friend—Calvin! I could feel a smile returning to my face.

Before I left the store, I picked out some special cards. Then I bought a package of cheap ones for most of the kids at school and headed for home.

That afternoon I had just gotten back from jogging when Sara called. "Did you have a good time?" I asked. I mean, the words just came flowing out, and they sounded warm and friendly!

"Katie, I'll never forget this day as long as I live!" she said.

"Want to come over and tell me about it?" I asked. I giggled. "I was going to offer to make hot chocolate! But would you settle for a diet Coke?"

"I'll be right over!" Sara said. "And please make hot chocolate! Katie, did you know it isn't healthy for kids our age to diet?"

We sat in front of the wood stove. Sara, unusually quiet, couldn't stop smiling.

"So tell me all about it," I said. "Did you eat in the greenhouse?"

She nodded. "Actually, we sat there the whole time!"

I was surprised. "You mean you didn't see the ice skating or the lake?"

"I saw the lake from a distance," Sara said. "Mostly we just talked. Katie, it was incredible! I mean, M. didn't even treat me like a child! It's the first time in my life a woman ever really talked to me!"

I smiled. "So, what did you talk about?"

"Everything!" Sara said. "I felt like I could tell her anything and she wouldn't hate me or get on my case!"

"Anything you can tell me?"

"Sure! You already know most of it anyhow, Katie!" Sara said. She took a deep breath. "What I never realized was that God has *always* loved me—even before I moved here and met you! I mean, the real God—who made everything—actually made me! He thinks I'm special! Me! Sara Wilcox!"

I smiled. I remembered when I first started telling her about Jesus. And the first time she prayed.

She smiled too. "Why I'm so special that if I were the only person in the world, Jesus would still have died just for me!"

"Are you sure?" I asked.

"Positive," Sara said. "Mayblossom showed me in her Bible!"

I was starting to get goose bumps.

"It's funny, Katie," Sara continued. "I heard what you told me. But I always thought God loved you more than me! After all, you've known about Him all your life! I always felt like just an outsider!"

"But you don't feel like that anymore?" Now I was getting really excited!

"Mayblossom said I could have Jesus in my heart just like you do!" She smiled. "You know, Katie, I think I'm ready to make some serious decisions about my relationship with Jesus."

"Sara," I said, "I'm so happy." I hugged her.

"And you know what?" she asked. "Mayblossom says the important thing isn't being cool on the outside! It's being cool on the inside!"

"At the rate you're going, Sara, you'll be teaching me before too long!" I laughed.

"That reminds me! I nearly forgot the best thing of all!" Sara said. "Mayblossom McDuff is going to be my new Sunday-school teacher!"

I was stunned. Suddenly, I was really tempted to start feeling jealous again! "Wow!" I said. "Maybe they'd let me transfer into your class!"

"Wouldn't that be cool!" Sara said.

For a while we just sat there and drank our

hot chocolate. I'll admit it was hard getting used to the idea that Jesus is as real to Sara as He is to me! And then I found myself wondering how Sara will change. Will she still be so much fun?

"It's a whole new me!" Sara said with her same old dramatic flair. Then her eyes got big. "Don't tell anybody, Katie, but I'm considering giving up my acting career! I think I'll become an author!"

"No kidding," I said. "Can you write?"

"We'll find out!" she laughed. "Actually, I'm planning to be just like Mayblossom McDuff! Katie, can't you just see me driving around in a little red sports car?"

"Maybe you wouldn't get a red sports car," I said. "Not all authors do, you know!"

"All right then, a *blue* sports car!" she laughed. "Blue is cool too!"

A Special Birthday

Happy Birthday to you!
Happy Birthday to you!
Happy Birthday, dear Katie!
Happy Birthday to you!

At first I thought I was dreaming! But then I realized that my family really was standing in my room holding candles and singing!

"Wake up, Sleepy Head!" Jason laughed. "I don't know about you, but I have to go to school!"

I sat up in bed and rubbed my eyes. "What a surprise!"

"It was your mother's idea," Dad laughed. "Personally, I thought you could wait until supper!"

"I wanted you to have this to wear today!" Mom said. She turned on the light. There, on a hanger, was the most beautiful red dress I've ever seen!

"You made that for me?"

Mom laughed. "Then you are surprised? When I found this material with hearts all over it, it just said *Katie Hooper* loud and clear! But I was afraid you saw me working on it. That's why I couldn't help you girls start your quilts."

"Katie, here's something I got you," Jason said. "You might want this now also!"

"I can save it until supper!" I said. That's when our family usually opens our birthday presents.

"Go on, open it!" Dad said.

I'm afraid I squealed! I couldn't believe it! It was a hair dryer! "Thanks, Jason!"

He smiled. "I thought it might help with your new hair style!"

"Katie will be the prettiest girl in school!" Dad said. "Now let's let her get dressed! Family breakfast in half an hour!"

Today I didn't hesitate. After my shower, I put on white tights and my good shoes. Even though I felt pretty clumsy with the hair dryer, my hair turned out great! And somehow the white collar on my dress really framed my face and hair.

When I entered the kitchen, my family cheered! "If you don't mind, Katie, I'll just sketch you now while you eat," Dad said.

"Just don't show me chewing!" I laughed.

I hated to wear a jacket over my dress, but of course I had to. I did skip the hat!

"Wait, Katie!" Mom called. "Your valentines!"

I rushed back, picked up the bag, and gave Mom a kiss. "Thanks!" I said. "What a surprise!"

"New dress?" Sara asked. Naturally she could see it hanging down beneath my jacket.

I smiled. "Mom made it for my birthday. See all the little hearts?"

"If it isn't Katie Hooper—my real live valentine!" Calvin gave me his biggest smile. "I'll be loving you always!" he sang.

I grinned. It was just like old times!

"I got Mr. Campbell a valentine," Sara said on the bus. "I wonder if Ms. Allen got him one?"

That's right! I remembered that this was the day Ms. Allen has been waiting for! Would she be wearing her ring? Would she tell the kids today? "I think she has a big surprise for Mr. Campbell!" I said.

Well, the first thing I did when I got into homeroom was to look at Ms. Allen's left hand. She wasn't wearing a ring. However, her smile lit up the room! "Happy Birthday, Katie!" she said. "What a beautiful dress! This afternoon you'll have to deliver our valentines!"

Everybody loved my dress! At least all the

girls did! By noon every single one of them had told me how nice I looked. Kimberly Harris even wondered if I'd come home with her sometime to show her mother! This was turning out to be the best day of my life!

For our class party, we had cupcakes with little red hearts stuck on top! Sue Capelleti's mother brought them. We also had red fruit punch, which led to Calvin's biggest burp of the month! Ms. Allen laughed harder than most of the kids.

When it was time to pass out the valentines, Ms. Allen said I could choose a boy to help me. I picked Robert Jackson because everybody knows I can't stand him. So I knew I wouldn't get teased or anything. Since I was so busy delivering valentines, I didn't have time to open mine. But I did have the impression that I got as many as anyone else did!

"So, how was your party?" Sara asked.

"Perfect!" I said. "This is probably my very best birthday!"

"Would you mind coming over to my house for a minute?" Sara asked. "I forgot something."

I couldn't believe how slow she was! "Katie, I think we should weigh ourselves!" she said. "Let's see how we're doing!"

Frankly, I wasn't too thrilled. But Sara was already in her stocking feet.

"I'm just the same!" Sara said. "Now, it's your turn!"

I stepped on the scale and looked. I couldn't believe it! I had lost a pound!

"Katie!" Sara grinned. "It's a miracle!"

"Maybe it's the jogging!" I smiled as I put on my shoes. "Sara, how come you're wearing your good shoes?"

"The other ones hurt my feet!" she said.

"Whoever heard of old jogging shoes hurting your feet!" I said.

At last we headed back to my house. "Oh, look!" I said. "There's Wimsey!" I opened the kitchen door, but I didn't see Mayblossom. After dumping my stuff on the table, I started through the house.

Suddenly I heard squeals and screaming! "Surprise! Surprise!" I couldn't believe it! The keeping room was full of people! *Happy Birthday, Valentine!* said a huge sign over the fireplace. Red and white balloons were hung all over. Near the doorway and next to my mother stood Mayblossom McDuff. And there was Pam O'Grady! And Sue Capelleti! Why, all the girls from my room at school were here!

"Mom!" I said.

"Don't look at me!" she laughed. "Mayblossom planned the whole thing!"

I ran over to M. and hugged her. "I heard you

never had a real birthday party," she said. "I thought it was about time we did something about that! And Sara was lots of help!"

"I feel like I'm dreaming!" I said. "Thanks!"

Well, M. thought of everything! There were games and prizes. And pink ice cream and angel food cake with pink frosting. And everybody got a ceramic heart-shaped box to take home.

"Katie, were you surprised?" asked Kimberly.

"Are you kidding?" I laughed. "I've never been so surprised in my life!"

The kids even brought me birthday presents! Pam gave me a stuffed bear. And Jennifer gave me some dusting powder. Kimberly gave me note paper with my name on it. Michelle gave me a book. And Sue gave me a darling pin shaped like a heart.

"What in the world?" I opened the next gift and pulled out a pair of pink jogging shoes! I finally found the card. It said, "To Katie Hooper, the best friend in the entire world! Love, Sara!"

"If they aren't the right size, we can take them back," Sara said.

With tears in my eyes, I turned to hug her. Now Sara was crying too. We both just stood there for a minute.

"There's one more box!" M. said, smiling. She handed me a large package covered with hearts.

Slowly I pulled off the paper and lifted the lid.

I could see something pink. "Oh, no! I can't believe it!" I said.

Inside was a beautiful pink velour jogging suit! The card said: "For my very special friend, Katie Hooper!" It was signed, "Love always, M."

After the party was over, several mothers came to pick up the girls. "How did you get here?" I asked.

"Uncle Sam drove us!" Sue said.

"Who's Uncle Sam?"

"Uncle Sam Johnson! Oh, Katie, I forgot you're new in town! Everybody in Woodland Park knows Uncle Sam!" she said. "He's a white-haired man who does all our plumbing. He's cool, but he doesn't talk much!"

"Silent Sam!" I laughed.

"I have to go home too, Katie," Sara said. "My mother is actually coming home for supper! Don't faint, but I'm fixing it!"

"I'm fainting," I laughed. "Hot dogs?"

"You guessed," she giggled. "But I'm also fixing peas and a salad!"

"Jell-O?" I teased.

"Are you kidding!"

After Sara left, I turned to Mom and M. "The girls were describing Silent Sam!" I said. "But how did he know about this?"

Mayblossom smiled. "Katie, I told you people who don't talk a lot sometimes have secrets!"

"You told him about my party?"

"Actually, Sam was very glad to help me out!" she said. Then, as I watched, suddenly her face turned pink!

"Mayblossom," I asked, "How was your steak fry?"

"Nice," she said, smiling. "In fact, it was very nice!"

I Run Into a Friend

The next afternoon, I couldn't wait to tell Sara all about Ms. Allen! "And her ring is really spectacular!" I said. "It's got to be the biggest diamond I ever saw!"

"The guy must be rich!" Sara said.

"She's so happy!" I smiled. "I guess her name isn't going to be Ms. Allen much longer! It'll be Mrs. McMann! They're getting married right after school's out!"

"Is she still going to teach fifth grade?"

"I really don't know," I said.

"Tell me again how Mr. Campbell fits into the picture."

"Your teacher's wife is Kevin McMann's sister!" I explained.

"I can't believe you actually met him!" she said. "How come you didn't tell me?"

"I promised," I told her.

Sara understood. "Katie, I just realized something! This is even more romantic than most soaps! Imagine getting an engagement ring on Valentine's Day! What a guy!"

That reminded me of something. "Sara, thanks for your help with my birthday party yesterday!" I said. "I sure was surprised!"

"I know," Sara smiled. "You should have seen the look on your face!"

We had reached my house. "Are you sure you don't want to go jogging with me this afternoon?" I asked. "I promise I'll take it slow until you get used to it!"

Sara smiled. "Thanks, but no thanks! When it comes to exercise, I'm just a couch potato! Maybe I'll practice my hemming! Otherwise we'll never get our quilts made!"

"There's really no rush!" I said. "Mom always says that actually *doing* something is more fun than *having it done!*"

"Katie, are you going to wear your shoes and that gorgeous new jogging suit?"

"I think I'll save the suit," I said. "I'd hate to wreck it or something!"

"Katie, live a little!" Sara said. "What are you saving it for—Amy?"

I grinned. "You're right! Thanks, Sara!"

"I'll call you after supper!" she said. "Have fun!"

I've never worn anything as soft and cuddly as my jogging suit. In fact, by the time I was dressed, I felt like I belonged on a shelf in somebody's stuffed animal collection!

Today my dog stood and whined as I tied my shoes. I think he's starting to enjoy this as much as I do! "All set, January!" I said. "Let's go!"

I took it slow and steady. Now I can jog a long time before I get out of breath. As we passed the old barn, I smiled. I wondered how much farther I could go.

Actually, I almost didn't see him. "Katie! Is that you?" It was Christopher Bean.

"I can't stop now," I gasped.

"OK if I join you?" He began to trot by my side. I nodded. I couldn't talk. The only sounds came from our feet pounding along together.

"Whew!" I said, finally, as I plopped down by the side of the road. It was hard to talk. "I really didn't think I could do it!"

Christopher sat down beside me. "You ran all the way from the other side of the barn?"

I nodded.

"I'm impressed, Katie!" He smiled. "You really have been working out, haven't you!"

I nodded again. Gradually my breathing

slowed down. "How come you're running over here? I thought you found a new place!"

"You want to know the truth?" He grinned.

"Sure."

Christopher kind of wiggled his foot. "The truth is, I was hoping I'd see you!"

"No kidding!" I said.

"No kidding!"

I didn't know what to say. I guess he didn't either, because we just sat there. The funny thing was that it wasn't really too embarrassing.

"Here comes your dog!" Christopher said. "I sure hope he doesn't howl!"

We both kind of held our breath as we watched January run toward us. Then he stopped and began to wag his tail. I grinned. "He likes you!"

"That's a relief!" Christopher said.

"Do you run every day?"

"Nearly," he said. "How about you?"

"Nearly," I told him. "Actually, I've been trying to get Sara to come with me, but she doesn't seem interested."

"Calvin doesn't either." After a moment of silence, he looked at me and smiled. "Maybe we could run together, Katie! When I said that before, I meant it!"

"You did?"

He grinned. "Actually, I wanted to call and

tell you that the night I first saw you running. As a matter of fact, I did call Sara to find out your phone number. But I was so nervous, I forgot to ask her for it. And then I was too embarrassed to call her back!"

"No kidding!" I said.

"No kidding!"

"I've always thought running would be even more fun if I had somebody to talk to afterwards! Somebody besides January, that is." I smiled. "I'd like to run with you, Christopher!"

"That's a relief!" He grinned. "Then it's a deal?"

I grinned too. "It's a deal!"

Now he seemed less nervous. "I like your outfit!" he said.

"Thanks!" I said. "I got it for my birthday!"

"It must be cool to have a birthday on Valentine's Day!"

"When's yours?"

"It's a really dumb time!" he said. "It's July 17!"

"That isn't dumb!" I said. "Every birthday's special! That's what my Mom always says!"

He stopped smiling. "I wish I had a mother!"

"What happened to her?" I asked.

"Divorced. She's in California."

"Oh."

"You're lucky to live with both your parents!"

I smiled. "You'll have to come and meet my family!" I said. "You'll like them. And I know they'll like you!"

"I already met your parents," he said. "Wasn't that your father who went on the field trip up Pikes Peak?"

"Of course!" I smiled. "I forgot!"

"And your mother was there when we ate all those cookies!"

I laughed. "I remember! The time I forgot my spelling book!"

He laughed too. "I didn't remember about the spelling book! Those were some cookies!"

Suddenly I realized it was getting dark! I wondered how long we had been talking. "I'd better start back," I said.

Now Christopher and I stopped talking. We just ran. But it was nice jogging along together. We got all the way to the back of our land. "I'm glad I ran into you, Christopher!" I said. "Or did you run into me?"

He laughed too. "Meet you here tomorrow?"

"Right!" I said. "We can decide the time after school."

He gave me a big smile, then turned and headed off.

"Katie, you look terrific!" Mom said, when I walked into the kitchen. "Your cheeks are as pink as your jogging suit!"

140

"Thanks." I couldn't stop smiling. "By the way, I have a new friend! Remember Christopher? Christopher Bean?"

But I didn't wait for her reply. Suddenly, I thought of something and ran upstairs to my room. I pulled out my valentines and began sorting through the pile. In the excitement of my birthday, I hadn't really taken time to read them carefully.

Here it was! The card showed a bear carrying his skis. He must have had an accident, because he was all bandaged up. I looked inside. It said:

I've fallen for you!
Be mine!

It was signed simply "Christopher."

Well, what do you know! Smiling, I tacked the valentine up on my bulletin board.